Requiem for
Na'aman

Requiem for Na'aman

by
Benjamin Tammuz

TRANSLATED BY MILDRED BUDNY AND
YEHUDA SAFRAN

NAL BOOKS
NEW AMERICAN LIBRARY
TIMES MIRROR
NEW YORK AND SCARBOROUGH, ONTARIO

Published simultaneously in Canada by
The New American Library of Canada Limited

SIGNET, SIGNET CLASSICS, MENTOR, PLUME, MERIDIAN AND
NAL BOOKS are published *in the United States* by The New
American Library, Inc., 1633 Broadway, New York,
New York 10019, *in Canada* by The New American Library
of Canada Limited, 81 Mack Avenue, Scarborough,
Ontario M1L 1M8

NAL BOOKS TRADEMARK REG. U.S. PAT. OFF. AND FOREIGN COUNTRIES
REGISTERED TRADEMARK—MARCA REGISTRADA
HECHO EN HARRISONBURG, VA., U.S.A.

Library of Congress Cataloging in Publication Data

Tammuz, Benjamin, 1919-
Requiem for Na'aman.

Translation of: Reḳvi em le-Na'aman.
I. Title.
PJ5054.T317R413   1982   892.4'36   81-22382
ISBN 0-453-00417-2   AACR2

Designed by Alan Steele

First Printing, June, 1982

1 2 3 4 5 6 7 8 9

PRINTED IN THE UNITED STATES OF AMERICA

PUBLISHER'S NOTE

This novel is a work of fiction. Names, characters, places, and incidents are either the product of the author's imagination or are used fictitiously, and any resemblance to actual persons, living or dead, events, or locales is entirely coincidental.

For Yishai Shachar

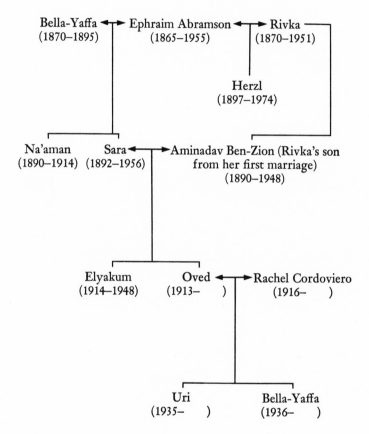

Requiem for Na'aman

1.

AMONG THOSE WHO commit suicide, the fortunate ones come by paper and pencil at their side at the decisive moment, and they write to us and explain to us; and although we will never make peace or agree with this, nevertheless the circle has somehow been closed and one can say that there has been no neglect or omission. But the unfortunate suicides are those who become so confused in their minds that instead of writing to us they speak to themselves, imagining that their words reach us, for we are, after all, their dear ones. Though it is not in malice that they do so, in the end the link connecting the dead with the living will be missing; and without this link—precarious as it may be—whence will culture grow?

1

2.

THERE WAS A woman in our settlement, during the Nineties of the previous century, named Bella-Yaffa,* and her husband's name was Froyke-Ephraim† and they had a son and a daughter, Na'aman and Sarah, and seventeen acres of cereal crops and six acres of almond trees and vines with a house, a stable, and a cow shed, and in the yard there were pigeons and chickens and kitchen vegetables planted behind the cow shed.

At night the moon pours its greenish light upon the yard, and the scraps of iron and wood scattered about move and whirl like living creatures, and the woman Bella-Yaffa leans on the porch rail, and is silent, and her husband works in the kitchen, and he too is silent, from experience; and some time later he comes out and places a hand on his wife's shoulder, to lead her to the bedroom, and then the woman says, "Look, Froyke, what magic there is all around us, what dreadful sadness."

And the husband says, "Bella, what, what will become of the children?"

Bella and *Yaffa* both mean "beautiful."

†*Froyke* is the Russian-Yiddish diminutive for the Hebrew *Ephraim*.

3.

AT THE END of that year, in the autumn, about a week before the High Holy Days, when the husband went to the Council House to examine accounts, Bella-Yaffa placed a saddle on the white stallion and rode out of the settlement. Schoolchildren later related that they had seen her riding toward the wadi.

In the early evening she crossed the plain of Sharon and rode north all night. Before dawn she reached a hilly place with wadis, and there she tied the stallion to a hedge of acacia trees and continued on foot toward cover at the foot of the hill. When the sky began to clear Bella-Yaffa saw, through the heaps of stones, several trees and a rocky slope closing the horizon. She made an effort to remember the names of the trees but could not. Then from her bag she took the bottle she had brought with her and drew out the cork.

4.

AND THESE ARE the words the woman spoke to her husband and children:

"I try to remember when the beginning was. Maybe

when I was five or six, when my father took me by cart to a wedding in a neighboring village. We left the city in the morning and for the first time in my life I saw open spaces, fields the color of gold, and avenues of slender trees, their trunks white with black stains, slender trees running like naked ghosts into infinity. I burst out crying and my father took me in his arms and hid my face inside his coat and whispered to me, 'Don't look at this defilement, Bella. It's a false charm, a vanity of the Gentiles. One of these days we'll get out of here and go to the land of our fathers. . . . There you'll see real trees, cedars of Lebanon. . . . The Redemption is not far off. . . . Another year or two, with God's grace, and our feet will tread on the soil of the destroyed sanctuary. . . .'

"When we returned from the wedding I had a fierce yearning to come back to those fields again, to run with the slender trees, the trembling and fluttering birches, and to vanish, together with them, into those terrible expanses my father had cursed. And at the same time I understood that if I really were to run with the trees, I would myself reach those mountains of cedars, without having to wait a year or two, which seemed to me like eternity. . . . Froyke, my dear, you brought me to the land of my father's dreams and I am requiting you with evil for good. . . . Why did you never ask me why I mixed poison in the cup of salvation? Why did you love me, despite my being so evil? If you had asked, if you had had the desire to hear, I would have told you. . . . You are so happy, toiling in the fields and vineyards,

4

rejoicing in your children, forgiving a wife who walks around your house like a ghost, in the house in which you serve as both father and mother, to both me and the children together. . . . And I, where am I going? That first revelation, riding with my father in the cart, was the first and the last. Add to it the songs which my ears absorbed in that country. . . . Add to it the names of the flowers and the trees, which I knew and whispered in my sleep. . . . Where are those cedars, Froyke? Now, beside this ruin, I see trees I don't know, and I will never know their names. . . . It may be that our forefathers, the ancient men of the desert, knew their names—but I don't know them. It's impossible to know things that came to an end thousands of years ago. It's possible to love only what has grown close to your bare feet, in the dawn of your childhood, Froyke. I suspect that you're lying, Froyke, when you seem to love this wilderness. . . . But how can I say that to you, when you look so happy, strong, pouring the sweat of your brow on the ominous rocks around the small and alien house you built with your own hands, a house without a thatched roof or a clay oven, without a chimney. . . .

"Forgive me, Froyke, my heart burns with a yearning for the place my father cursed so vigorously. . . . Had you spoken to me and asked me, I might have told you that the destroyed sanctuary, the dream my father left me, may perhaps become our children's lot. . . . As for me, my soul longs for the dream, but I sense that it dwells beyond the place to which those birches ran like

5

mad, and I also am going there, perhaps in order to be with you and the children at last . . . to be truly, whole-heartedly, forever. Froyke, my love, I love the dream more than I love you. . . . I am a soul struck off from the book of life. Remember me, Froyke, kiss the children. . . . They're little, they'll forget me."

5.

THE WOMAN DREW the cork from the bottle and for a moment a sour and moldy smell rose to her nostrils, like the smell hovering about the shed at the back of the yard when Froyke-Ephraim soaks the almond-shells in water, as fodder for the cattle. For a moment the woman seemed to have gone back on her decision, but then she quickly lifted the bottle to her lips and drank the liquid to the last drop. She lay down on her back and from the corner of her eye saw the sun rising over the slope. Then fierce pains attacked her in her stomach, and through gritted teeth she emitted some shouts mingled with words in a foreign language. An old vineyard watchman, an Arab from a nearby village, heard her cries and drew near to where she lay. He leaned over the woman, who was now whispering and sobbing, and a sour smell rose to his nose. He had never seen a Jewish woman drunk, and the thing was a wonder in his eyes. At first he tried to revive her by waving his hand, to bring some of the morning breeze to her nostrils, but when he saw her closing her eyes and falling asleep, illicit thoughts came to him. Bella-Yaffa was twenty-five years old when she died, with a perfect beauty, as her husband would remember her to his dying day.

When the old Arab realized that the woman was dead, he dragged some stones of the place and covered her corpse, until the pile could not be distinguished from all the other heaps of rubble all around.

6.

WHEN FROYKE-EPHRAIM came back from the Council House and found the children crying, he made them a meal and went to the cow shed and from there to the stable. And in the stable he found that the white stallion was gone. Only in the evening did he hear from the schoolchildren that they had seen the woman riding toward the wadi. Immediately the man set out in the same direction, on a borrowed horse. Two neighbors rode out too, one to the west, to the seashore, and the other to the east, to the hills. All three returned toward morning, exhausted and stunned. That day they sent messengers to the Jewish settlements in Judea, Samaria, and Galilee, where they bribed Turkish gendarmes to keep their eyes and ears open and report back about what they saw and heard, and they also sent a letter to the newspaper *Ha-*

Levanon in Jerusalem, asking the editors to print a notice to the public about the woman whose traces had vanished.

The High Holy Days came and went, the first rains descended and the earth was plowed in readiness for the sowing. After Passover Froyke-Ephraim reaped his field and bound his sheaves and at the beginning of the summer journeyed to the Chief Rabbi to ask him for permission to take another wife, the widow of a farmer killed some six months earlier. The Chief Rabbi was hesitant, and said that according to the strict rule of justice the law permitted it, but that according to the merciful approach to justice it would be proper to wait.

Upon hearing this Froyke-Ephraim became enraged and shouted, "Leave the merciful approach to justice to me, Honored Rabbi. My heart is broken as it is."

And Froyke-Ephraim found himself another rabbi, in Jaffa, who agreed to conduct the wedding immediately after Bella-Yaffa was declared divorced.

The widow, a strong and merry woman named Rivka, brought him as dowry a five-year-old boy, named Aminadav, seventeen acres of cereal crops, six acres of vines and almond trees, a house with a piano and also a cow shed, but no stable. Rivka had sold the pair of horses after her husband's death to maintain herself and her son Aminadav. And since Froyke-Ephraim's white stallion had also been lost, as is known, one letter was sent to Paris, to Baron Rothschild, and another letter to Odessa, to the Council which supported Jewish settlement in the

Land of Israel, both letters containing thorough explanations that allotments of thirty-four acres of cereal crops could not be worked without horses.

The Baron and the Council in Odessa replied as they replied.

In time Na'aman, Froyke-Ephraim's first son from his first marriage, began to strike upon the piano which his stepmother had brought to the house.

7.

AFTER FROYKE-EPHRAIM brought the woman Rivka to his house, the Council of the settlement convened an extraordinary session, and there tempers flared up violently. In particular their anger turned against the Jaffa rabbi who had permitted the marriage. They called him a hypocrite, for only some six months earlier he had forbidden the staging of a theatrical performance by Jews in Jaffa, because he had found arguments in the Gemarah* that theaters were idolatry. That being so, whence had he the authority to permit an immediate marriage between a widow and a man whose wife had vanished without trace?

If the truth be told, the farmers had never liked Bella-

---

*The second, concluding section of the Talmud, supplying a commentary on the first part, the Mishnah.

Yaffa. It can be said that they had hated her in their hearts. But people fight for a principle more than they give themselves over to the love of others, because a principle is hatred of the opponent.

But before the vote was taken it was decided to invite Froyke-Ephraim to the meeting, so that he could say what he had to say in his defense.

And these are the words that Froyke-Ephraim spoke in their presence:

"Gentlemen and my brother farmers, first of all let me inform you that I am speaking on behalf of two plots of cereal crops and two plots of vines and almond trees, from which the intelligent will easily grasp that I have two votes in any count. And secondly, consider that it was not for the love of women or the lust of the flesh that I brought a new wife into my house. Only the redemption of the land lay before my eyes, and how can I bear to see the fields turn fallow and desolate because I don't have a woman in the house to give a hand with raising the children, milking the cows, and doing the kitchen work? My brother farmers, was it not to work the land that we came to the land of our fathers? Is not working the land considered equal to worshiping the Creator? And who am I to dispute the decision of the rabbi from Jaffa? I am a farmer, a tiller of the soil, not a sage learned in the Torah. Please, my friends, consider this and do not betray our common goal, the exalted aim of regenerating the wastes of the Land of Israel and of restoring the dispersions of our people, to bring them back to our land, a land flowing with milk and honey. And God who dwells on high, He shall look down upon us from His height of heights, and He will judge, for it is for Him to judge and for us to do the work."

Thus spoke Froyke-Ephraim on that day, and the farmers listened and remained silent a long while. Finally they gave up the vote and it was decided that if one day a master in the Torah happened to come to the settlement, they would place the matter before him. And on his part Froyke-Ephraim promised that if Bella-Yaffa, the woman who had vanished, were found, he would restore her honorably to her place in his house, and would also adopt the second woman, Rivka, into his household, as the rabbis would decree, without depriving her, God forbid, of her share in the fields and vineyards which she had brought him as a dowry.

And life returned to normal and the present was not distinguishable from the past. Only he who sees into the heart knows that Froyke-Ephraim did not forget Bella-Yaffa, and at night he saw her in his dreams and spoke to her words of entreaty and love.

8.

ABOUT A YEAR and a half after these events, the First Zionist Congress took place in the city of Basel, in Switzerland, and there appeared the man whom many saw as the king of the Jews, in other words, Doctor Benjamin Ze'ev Theodor Herzl. And when a male child was born to Froyke-Ephraim and Rivka, they named him Herzl, and on the day that they celebrated his circumcision, Froyke-Ephraim made a speech. The Secretary of the Council wrote down the speaker's words, and they are recorded in the register of the settlement, and if it has not been eaten by moths, or burned in fires, and if its pages were not scattered in the pogroms that the Arabs wrought upon the settlement, and if it did not rot in the rains when the Turks refused the settlers permission to put a roof on the new Council House which they had built without a permit, then his words are still inscribed there for generations to come, in eternal remembrance.

Such was the surface of things, stormy on the outside. But within, the streams of life flowed serenely and tranquilly, as befitted the lives of settlers. The changes took place according to the seasons of the year and shifting agricultural requirements, and if something happened that digressed from this cycle, the farmers were startled to see that not one year had passed, but seven or ten. And a man would say to his neighbor: Look, ha!—and I didn't know.

So it was when, all of a sudden, Froyke-Ephraim's sister came from the settlement in Sharon, mounted on a mule, alone. She dropped from the beast, climbed the wooden steps of the porch, and fell upon her brother's neck, weeping. And when she had caught her breath she sat down at the table, sipped the tea Rivka had brought her, and told her story.

Requiem for Na'aman

At the end of the previous summer her husband had been found killed, stabbed with a dagger, in the new citrus grove. At the beginning of the winter her two daughters had died of malaria, they being the last of the children remaining alive in the settlement, apart from her little son. From then on only the older people and the younger son remained. After that fathers and mothers started dying, elderly people and even bachelors. At the end of the winter the little son died too. "I didn't let them bury him," said Froyke-Ephraim's sister, "until I had settled accounts with the One who sits on high. I stood at the window with the child in my arms, and I said to Him, 'Well, now are You happy? . . .' He didn't answer me, and what could He have answered? . . . Froyke, here I am in your house, and if you don't want me, turn me away. . . ."

Tears dropped from Froyke-Ephraim's eyes and Rivka embraced his sister by the shoulders and said to her, "Abide with us, our house is your house; but I can offer no solace with my words. . . . What the Lord has done to you, only He has the solutions thereof."

Froyke-Ephraim struck the table with his fist, the tea in the glass leapt onto the tablecloth, and he got up and left the house. He returned only in the evening. He took his sister's face in his two hands and said to her, "He'll regret this, oh how He'll regret this."

And the streams of life continued flowing in their path, according to the seasons. Almond trees were uprooted and some of the fields where the earth was light became orchards of oranges, lemons, and citrons. And

13

when the orange trade boomed and oranges were transported in ships to the countries of Europe, Froyke-Ephraim bought new land, on which he also planted citrus trees. That year the Citrus-Growers' Association was founded, and Froyke-Ephraim was elected its president.

To the first house that Froyke-Ephraim and Bella-Yaffa had built two new wings were added. They contained rooms for the children—for Na'aman and Sarah, Bella-Yaffa's children, for Aminadav, Rivka's son by her first marriage, and for little Herzl, the son of Froyke-Ephraim and Rivka. A special room was also built for Froyke-Ephraim's sister.

When Sarah, Bella-Yaffa's daughter, turned fourteen, she resembled her mother in beauty and feminine comeliness, but her spirit was molded after her father's character. She knew her own will and imposed her authority on her surroundings.

And she loved Aminadav, her stepbrother, and without a word guided him into loving her. She never made spoken demands, but she always obtained her wish. And the fifteen-year-old Aminadav would help her with the housework, and since he was strong, like his mother, he willingly did as Sarah wished, from the day he came with his mother to live in Froyke-Ephraim's house.

Settlement youngsters are hot-blooded and know no inhibitions, like domestic animals and beasts of the field; and after Sarah drew Aminadav, in the middle of the day, to the empty stable, where the two of them tasted the fruit of the tree of knowledge, they did not leave off immersing themselves in each other at every suitable moment.

Once little Herzl was wandering around the yard and found his way to the stable. The sight that was revealed to him was a great wonder to him and he did not part his lips and he stood there in silence until Sarah and Aminadav noticed him. A glow lit up his face and he said to them, "Take me with you too."

Sarah told him that if he opened his mouth she would kill him for sure, but if he kept quiet they would include him in their company one day. Little Herzl promised and kept his promise.

And among the village pleasures and oddities, Na'aman, the son of Bella-Yaffa, was odd and even more peculiar. On the day that his stepmother had brought the piano to the house ten years before, he had struck its keys and had not stopped since then. Half the day he was at school, and the other half—whilst his sister and brother helped in the yard, in the house, or in the orchard—he would sit at the piano. Subsequently a teacher was found to assist him. She had learned to play in Odessa, before coming to the Land of Israel, and now she was glad to return a little to the life she had known in her youth. She was a melancholy woman, and the melodies she brought to Na'aman were strained, dismal, depressing to the spirit and bringing tears between the eyelashes. When she saw that her pupil's eyes also watered easily she rejoiced in him with great joy and

15

went on lugging scores by Glinka and Tchaikovsky, and a few melodies by Chopin, to the house until one day she saw that indeed her pupil had reached a stage at which she had nothing to add.

Froyke-Ephraim sensed and understood that Na'aman was his mother's son and had no place among farmers. If the father did not want any harm to befall his son, he would have to allow him to do his will. So it was agreed that Na'aman would go to Jerusalem, to study at the music school, and would return home for Passover and New Year's Day.

And so when he was sixteen Na'aman was uprooted from his father's house. In Jerusalem he lived in his teacher's house, and as he had not spoken much with others whilst living in his father's house, at his teacher's house he stopped talking completely, except for what was necessary to ask and to reply in connection with his studies. And when he had time off from studies he would walk beyond the houses outside the city wall, holding in his hand a notebook for musical notation, and he would write notes to himself in his copybook. And when he had walked until he was tired, he would sit down on a stone by the roadside and look at the firmament of stars, and his eyes would fill with tears.

Several years later, in Paris, he would think a lot about those nights in Jerusalem, and would say to himself that those were the most beautiful years of his life.

Requiem for Na'aman

9.

ABOUT TWO YEARS before the outbreak of the First World War, oranges from the Land of Israel became current stock-in-trade all over Europe. The prospering fruit growers convened an assembly and decided to send an emissary abroad, to make trade connections, establish a network of agents, and lease warehouses and ships.

Froyke-Ephraim accepted the burden of exile to the places of commerce, and told those gathered at the assembly that he accepted the decision of the Association, and was willing to submit himself to the torments of wayfaring on ships and trains, only if this would help to consolidate the economy of the Land of Israel, so that the nation dwelling in Zion could buy more land and thus strengthen the might of the young Jewish settlement until the Final Redemption. Envoys before him had gone out to the world from the Land of Israel, but they had gone to beg for alms, whilst Froyke-Ephraim was the first of the daring who took upon themselves the afflictions of exile for commercial purposes, which are the basic foundation for the building of the country through work and lofty ideals.

In that year the twenty-two-year-old Na'aman worked as a music teacher in Jerusalem. After completing his studies in the Academy he had not returned to his father's house, but lived in a rented room in Nahlat-Shiv'ah. Most of his time he would spend at the Academy, but a few select pupils would come to him in his room, affable youngsters from distinguished families, and apart from them Na'aman did not make friends with anyone. He never started a conversation with the girls at the Academy and he was in awe of them. But the youths, his pupils, he loved with a fierce love, secretly.

When Froyke-Ephraim went to Jerusalem to obtain a farewell blessing from his son, Na'aman disclosed to him that he yearned to go to Paris, where he longed to return to his studies. Na'aman was twenty-two, like his mother in his face, his movements, and his whispering speech; and the father looked at him for a long while and terrible thoughts flooded his heart, and a sudden fear gripped him.

And Froyke-Ephraim said, "Well, then, let's both of us go to Europe. You to Paris and I to London. . . . We'll take the same ship to Marseilles, Na'aman. What do you say to that?"

Na'aman lowered his eyes and said, "Thank you, Father."

Soon after Passover the two of them went down to Jaffa and sailed on a French ship to Marseilles, two years before the war.

10.

THE WOMAN RIVKA and her son from her first marriage, Aminadav, and Bella-Yaffa's daughter Sarah accompanied Froyke-Ephraim and his son Na'aman to the port; and when they returned on their own to the settlement Aminadav disclosed to his mother that Sarah had conceived by him, and that they were to be brought together in matrimony. So long as the father had been at home they had feared to disclose the matter to him, and now they ought to do what was to be done.

Rivka did not hesitate for long and agreed. By the time her husband came back from his trip Sarah's belly would tell the tale, and all talk would be needless.

The wedding took place on Lag Ba'Omer* and this time the astounded farmers did not convene an express Council meeting. By now they were accustomed to the oddities of this founding family, and what is more, Froyke-Ephraim was their emissary and the president of the Citrus-Growers' Association.

---

*The thirty-third day of reaping, a single day of festivity, when shaving and marriages are permitted, within the fifty days of mourning which follow Passover.

11.

ON THE FIRST night of their voyage, after they had finished supper, the father and the son took two deck chairs and sat down beside each other, in the dark, with their faces toward the sea.

Froyke-Ephraim, who had not seen his son for a year, was still struck by the boy's resemblance to his mother; and sitting in the darkness on the deck, he thought about that other voyage, when he had sailed with Bella-Yaffa from Odessa to Jaffa, thirty years before.

When the Messiah will come and we will see the resurrection of the dead—Froyke-Ephraim found himself musing, turning over in his mind thoughts of things which he had learned as a child and which lay in forgotten corners of his soul—when the Messiah will come and we will see the resurrection of the dead, what will be the judgment accorded a man who has had two wives? Who will be his wife, when the dead are resurrected to eternal life? Some say: When the Messiah will come all the commandments will be annulled, and even the families will be annulled and canceled out. And some say: His first wife—the first wife a man has had, and not the second.

And if I assume so—Froyke-Ephraim turned over an ancient incantation, one of the incantations of the House of Learning, the Beit-Ha-Midrash—and if I assume so, then suppose I am at this very moment in the midst of the Days of the Messiah, already after the resurrection of the dead . . . for here is Bella-Yaffa sitting already beside me, and if I only stretch out my hand I will be able to touch her.

He rose from his chair, and without glancing at his son walked over to the railing of the ship and stood there, and closed his eyes. A breeze caressed his face and tickled him under his thick mustache, and because of the tickling sensation and the smell of the sea and the saltiness of the air he blinked his eyes and blinked them again until a tear was squeezed out and then another and they dripped along his cheeks, and his ears too opened to some voice, some familiar song, remembered and not remembered, very close and very distant. He wiped his face with his hand and returned to the chair beside his son.

"Na'aman," he said, filling his voice with all the strength of his lungs, "Na'aman, after all you are a musician, and you know many songs. . . . Perhaps you know some song they used to sing when I was a boy, in Russia? . . . One of those accursed Gentile songs, sad, beautiful songs, damn it. . . . Do you know any sad Russian songs?"

"I can try, Father," said Na'aman. "Will you come down to the dining-room? There is a piano there."

The son led the way and the father followed, looking at his son from behind. The father's legs were a bit shaky, but in the rest of his body, especially in the chest, he felt a kind of excitement which recalled things long forgotten. He felt as though something lost might now return to its owner, be it only in a dream at night or in a silly delusion. He felt as if he were about to commit a transgression, to do something unworthy of a man of his stature, but the sweetness of the thing drew him, and anyway there were no witnesses here, except for his son, who did not really have the status of a witness, because he was the reincarnation of another soul and was equally compelled to commit the transgression. A disembodied soul.

Na'aman sat down at the piano and played a barcarole by Tchaikovsky, and Froyke-Ephraim sank into an armchair in the empty and half-dark dining room.

"That's like it," the father murmured, "but not quite . . . not quite. . . . Try something a little less learned . . . not a song of the intelligentsia, but something popular, Na'aman. Something from the village, from the people. . . . Surely you can try. . . . Don't despair. We're very close to the songs I want to hear."

Na'aman tried Glinka's "Doubts" and looked over his shoulder at his father, who nodded his head and whispered, "Don't stop. . . . That isn't it, but very close, very close. Play a bit more. Soon we shall reach our heart's desire."

Na'aman started playing "On the Threshold of the House," "Evening Chime," "My Fire Gleams in the Fog," and finally, smiling to himself, returned to Tchaikovsky and played "Whither, Whither Have You Gone, My Days," from *Eugene Onegin*.

Requiem for Na'aman

Na'aman stopped playing and the father was silent. The son's hands rested motionless on his knees and the father's hands rubbed, and kept on rubbing, the bristle on his unshaven cheeks. They sat in the darkened room at a distance of about ten paces from each other, and from the belly of the ship came the dull sound of the engine.

"Na'aman," said the father, "why haven't you ever asked me about your mother? After all, your mother vanished from our lives, like a ghost. . . . And you never asked me, even once."

"We've never talked, Father," said Na'aman from his seat at the piano, not turning his head.

"Are you blaming me, Na'aman?"

"You're the one who comes with complaints," said Na'aman. "I did not accuse you."

Again the engine of the ship continued to beat out the time and the silence between them, until finally Froyke-Ephraim took a deep breath and started to speak. At first he spoke in a whisper and then his voice rose and fell, like one who has no control over his mood.

"Your mother was twenty-five when she left me, and you were five years old at the time. . . . Seventeen years have passed since then, Na'aman, seventeen years, and I haven't had a single day, not a single day, do you hear, not one single day free of her memory. . . . True, I married another woman and Herzl was born to us, and I have no reproaches against this woman. . . . But know, Na'aman, that there is a dagger stuck in my heart, and it bleeds. You were still at home when I planted the first citrus orchard, but you didn't see a thing. . . . You were engrossed in your music. And I—when the workers finished bringing the saplings from the nursery—I said to them: Go from here, go and come back tomorrow. And I myself waited for it to become dark and I took the first sapling and went and dug a pit and planted the sapling in the ground and cried, 'Bella, my Bella. . . .' I wanted her to know that I was planting new trees on our estate. 'Bella,' I shouted like mad, 'Bella, why did you leave me?' But no one heard. . . . You were playing, and Sarah and Aminadav were probably in the stable. . . . I know everything about my family, Na'aman, don't think that I don't know. . . . And the good Rivka was washing clothes for you in the yard and no one would have heard. But your mother knows that I cry out to her at night. She knows, but she doesn't return. . . . For seventeen years she hasn't returned. . . . What, Na'aman, what do you think to yourself, what, Na'aman? That I'm leaving my farm and the settlement just like that and going on a ship only to do business in oranges? . . . I'm not saying that isn't important. . . . I'll do my work faithfully, no one need worry about that. But why am I going back to these accursed countries? I will tell you, Na'aman, why I travel. I am looking for my first wife. Perhaps she returned to Russia? Or perhaps she went on to England, or to France? Perhaps she has made a new tie. How could I know? Suddenly, with no notice whatsoever, she rose up and went . . . left a husband and a home and a little boy and a baby girl. . . . She was not one of those who suddenly leave their family. . . . So why, why, did she go? Na'aman, you're an educated man, answer me, Na'aman."

"I don't know, Father," said Na'aman from the piano, and his head still faced the keys.

"You don't know?" In Froyke-Ephraim's voice there could be heard such a great shock that it seemed as if he had said, "So to what purpose have I told you all these things?"

"How is it that you don't know?" the father repeated his question. "You're so much like her. . . . You have no idea, Na'aman, how much you are like your mother. . . . And now you too are traveling abroad and leaving me. . . . And I thought that if the desire to rise up and go has overwhelmed you, then you could also explain to me, to answer my question. . . ."

"I left home long ago, Father, and you never asked me even once," said Na'aman.

"But I'm asking you now," said Froyke-Ephraim impatiently.

"And I'm answering you: I don't know."

"Are you angry with me, Na'aman? Is there something in me that people have to escape from? You must explain it to me, you have to do this for me, to help me."

"How can I help you? I'm only in the beginning of my life." And this time Na'aman turned his head and looked his father straight in the face. "How can you demand this of me? Do you want to lay this whole burden on my shoulders? Do you think you're entitled to? Don't you think I have enough of my own? Enough and more than enough of my own?"

And then, suddenly, the intoxication in which the father had been immersed lifted. A thin stab, brief as the blinking of the eyelashes, penetrated his chest and evanesced. He looked at his son and fell silent.

12.

In Paris, on the sixth floor, in a small street leading to the river, Na'aman sat at the window and peeped out. He was afraid to go outside, because something terrible had happened to him, already on the very first day. Wherever he turned, from the moment he got off the train that had brought him from Marseilles, he saw sights known to him as familiar from the past. And it was not only the places which seemed to bring back forgotten memories, but also the smells and especially the voices. Not the voices of human beings, but the voices of things, the stones and the water, those voices jangling in the air; if you are not made for this, you do not hear them at all.

At first Na'aman was surprised, almost happy, and already prepared himself for a kind of celebration, apparently awaiting him here for many days. Leaning on the stone balustrade he looked at the water in the river, and the water sent him tiny tongues, sticking them out and hiding them, and said to him: Glock-lack-lick-lock, don't you wish, Na'aman, to share our luck?

And the stone under his elbow rustled and said: Ustle-ustle-us, go down, the steps are expecting you, to the water, water, water.

And when he turned away from there and set out toward the houses alongside the river there rose to his nose the smell of foods whose taste he knew. But who was it that had cooked them for him? It was not hunger that Na'aman felt from the smell of the dishes, but an undefined longing, a tugging yearning and a trembling in the flanks of his body. And then he knew in his heart that if he turned and entered the narrow alley opposite and then turned right, he would be standing opposite a white house with red shutters and on the second floor there would be lace curtains slightly parted and a familiar face peeping out from among the folds of the curtains. Whose face is that?—Na'aman tried to recall, and his heart skipped a beat.

He did not leave his room on the sixth floor, and his food was brought to him by the landlady, as agreed. And he sat at the piano and played, made marks in his composition notebook, and played again. Tears would pour down his cheeks, but a wry smile would also sprout and rise on his lips, for on hearing the melodies he had composed he became aware that he was circling around and around the melodies he had played for his father on the ship. The tune of "My Fire Gleams in the Fog"

27

began to stretch out arms to a distant region, expanding and embracing the starry skies of Jerusalem and returning from there to somewhere else, somewhere dark, moist, cold, with the sound of a bell behind his back.

And one day there was a knock on the door, and a heavily built man, with a thick mustache and heavy shoulders, stood in the entrance. Na'aman looked at the man entering and was silent. He was not alarmed, he was just expecting the man to vanish as he had come. He wanted to return to the piano and the bell.

"Na'aman," whispered the man who had entered, "why are you looking at me like that?"

And Na'aman said, "I am playing. I am tired, and I have been playing."

Froyke-Ephraim hired a carriage and took his son to a physician, and the physician prescribed medicines and assured the father that his son would recover his strength, that this was but a weakness, a weakness of the nerves, and that he would do well to travel to the bosom of nature, to live in the country for a while.

Then the father took his son to a restaurant and made him eat meat and fresh vegetables.

Upon their return to the room the father told his son that he had made numerous inquiries in the offices of the Jewish community in London, but had discovered nothing about Bella-Yaffa. From here he was going on to Odessa. His work in London had gone well and an office had already been opened there for the Citrus-Growers' Association of the Land of Israel.

Froyke-Ephraim promised his son that he would visit

him again on his way back from Russia, and made Na'aman swear that he would imbibe the medicines he had been prescribed, and would go out for walks in the parks and boulevards. And to Na'aman's landlady he gave specific instructions about the kind of foods that were to be prepared for his son, and gave her an increase on the rent.

13.

SUCCESS SHONE UPON Froyke-Ephraim. In London a reception was held in his honor at Zionist Federation House and Doctor Chaim Weizmann embraced him by the shoulders in front of the assembly, and said to those gathered there, "Here, gentlemen, look and behold what a figure the new Jew is in the Land of Israel."

And the public looked at Froyke-Ephraim's face and applauded.

"Ephraim Abramson," said Doctor Weizmann, "is the fulfillment of the promise which the Zionist movement gave to the Jewish people. He is a pioneer, he is strong, a tiller of the soil who sees blessing in his labor, a proud and powerful emissary who brings us the smell of the earth, the smell of the citrus in bloom. He brings not only that, but also an emphatic demand, a demand he makes of each one of us, to lend a hand in the consolidation of Jewish agriculture in the Land of Israel."

Many came to shake his hand, and several of those

who shook his hand also added, almost casually, that they would be glad to meet him in private, to discuss the matter for which he had come.

When Ephraim Abramson left London, on his way to Paris, he entertained himself with thoughts of the pleasant meeting with his son, when he would tell him about the magnificent occasion in London and about the honor which the Jews of the Diaspora had paid to a simple Jew from the Land of Israel.

In Paris Ephraim Abramson was the guest of one of the Baron's high officials and at his table he ate abominable food served up with much ado. In Paris too his affairs went well, but there too he did not discover anything, not one thing, about Bella-Yaffa, and instead of lingering in Western Europe, he was in haste to get to the land of Russia. Was not that where Bella-Yaffa had come from? Perhaps she had returned there, and there he might find her.

And indeed he did find and come upon people in Odessa who remembered his wife's family, but her parents had died and one of her brothers had emigrated to America. About the other members of the family they did not know anything to tell, beyond what they knew, that the daughter had married a man who had left for the Land of Israel many years ago.

"I am the man," said Ephraim, "and that daughter was my wife, and she is the one I'm looking for."

And the people shrugged their shoulders and said no more. But from that time on they began to suspect that Ephraim Abramson was not perfectly balanced in his mind and possibly he was not the man to do business with.

It was fortunate for him that he did business with the Gentiles in Odessa, with the city and port authorities, and kept away from the Jews of Odessa. And when he had completed his business he went by train to Kiev and Kharkov, where in times past some members of Bella-Yaffa's family had lived. In Kiev he found no trace of them, but in Kharkov he met a family of soap-makers, three brothers working in partnership, the youngest of whom had married the elder sister of Bella-Yaffa.

Before meeting his sister-in-law Ephraim visited a barber and had his mustache trimmed and asked for perfume to be sprayed on his hair; then he returned to his hotel and donned the same black suit in which he had appeared before Doctor Weizmann and his associates in London. In front of the mirror he drew himself erect and practiced several hand and arm gestures of grandeur and etiquette, and when he was satisfied with himself he walked very slowly to his sister-in-law's house, taking care not to get his clothes creased.

Bella-Yaffa's sister fell upon his neck with kisses, and even though she had never seen him in her life, received him like a member of the family. Even before he had uttered a word, the woman showered a stream of amiable complaints upon him, scolding him for not making her sister write letters, even if it might be a single little line, nothing, just to inform her about her health and her actions.

"It may be that Asiatics don't have the habit of writing," she said. "But you, nevertheless, are children of Europe, and even if you've forgotten this, I am still her sister, her own flesh and blood. Is it right to behave in such a manner, Mr. Abramson?"

"When, may I ask," said Ephraim, "did you receive your last letter from Bella?"

"When?" laughed the woman. "Perhaps twenty years ago. . . . What am I saying? More than twenty years ago."

"And since then—nothing?"

"Not a thing, I am telling you." And suddenly her face changed. "Tell me, has something terrible happened? I don't like the look on your face. I am frightened."

And Ephraim told her what he knew and Bella-Yaffa's sister sat down opposite him, her hands crossed in her lap, and wept. Tears which came a quarter of a century late, a woman's tears, which neither added nor detracted a thing from Ephraim's point of view.

When he took his leave of the family he promised to send photographs of the children, and told his brother-in-law that if he brought his family to the Land of Israel, he should come to him, and he promised that if he did, he would assist him in setting up a soap factory in the Land of Israel, where it would be the first Jewish soap factory since the days when the prophet said, "For though thou wash thee with niter, and take thee much soap, . . ." and so on and so forth.

Then he left the house, walked along the alley called

the Alley of the Pharmacies, and came out into Sum-
skaya Street. He remembered several indistinct things,
but instead of straining his memory he emitted a curse,
and vowed to himself that from now on his foot would
not tread again on foreign soil. From this day forward he
would stay at home and would not take on any mission.

14.

WHEN EPHRAIM LEFT Paris and Na'aman remained alone
in his room, he sat down at the piano, looked at the keys,
and realized that they were mute. There would be no
point in striking them again. For a long while he sat
looking straight ahead, and afterward he covered the
keys with a strip of felt, shut the wooden lid, got up,
made a bow, mumbled several words of apology, and
left the room.

The many sounds that rose from the street did not
combine in a melody. They scattered and broke, grating
on his ear until he felt pain in his eardrums.

In Jerusalem—Na'aman remembered—even the stillness of the night would join in a melody. Even the silence of the stars would offer itself to his ears as a kind
of song, and he would even note it down in his notebook.
Here, on the other hand, the piano keys had also turned
mute, the sounds of the city all the more so, and if they
were not mute, they hurt and pained him.

Nevertheless he knew, beyond the shadow of a doubt, that even if he returned to Jerusalem he would no longer hear the melody, because the ducts leading in from the outside had been damaged; and the vessels leading out from the inside had burst and become distended, and were now torn and bleeding without restraint. He listened to the flow, the slow incessant outpouring from inside out, emptying him as he walked, sinking, without complaint, into a silent being.

He knew that if he found a bracket to hold on to, he might be saved; and he sought something to hold on to, passing in his mind's eye through the landscape in which such a bracket could be found.

The house in the settlement in the south was an empty void, wholly inhabited by the absence of his mother. In Jerusalem several of his former students had given up the piano and taken up wives, apparently. Na'aman had never made any other offer to them. He had expected them to understand, and they did not understand. And as for his father, he was a big mountain, a mountain rising in the wilderness, and the current in which Na'aman was being swept along skirted the mountain at dizzying speed and flowed on toward the valleys, down, around, and far away.

There was no use in screaming from within the current. The sound of the water was strong and the mountain was high and deaf.

Na'aman leaned his back against the wall of a house, looked at the summer street, at the passersby. He was smiling. A young woman came up to him, took a hand-kerchief from her purse, wiped his face and spoke to him. He identified her as a G-minor that kept on smiling. She shoved a slice of chocolate into his mouth, and he emitted it with a spit.

Toward morning, in his room, lying on the bed with his eyes closed, he made an effort to remember who was the young woman he had met in the street; and after a great effort, perhaps only by noon, he thought she was his mother. Tomorrow—or perhaps even this very evening—he would return to the same place and wait for her. Evening after evening he would go there, until she would return.

15.

ABOUT THREE MONTHS following the day when Ephraim had visited his son in Paris, he returned and stood in the doorway of the room on the sixth floor. He knew that each month money arrived from the bank and was paid in part to the landlady and in part to Na'aman. He also remembered the physician's assurance that choice food and strolls in the parks would restore his son's health. He therefore hoped only for good, but fear nested hidden in his heart.

When Ephraim opened the door he saw before him a young man whose hair had grown like a woman's hair.

A sparse beard, like the beards of boys who have never shaved, covered his cheeks with a pale down and drooped from the tip of his chin. His cheeks were gaunt, with a sickly flush upon them, and his eyes burned with a strange fire. Na'aman was standing in the middle of the room and on seeing his father made a bow and stretched his arms to the sides, as if apologizing.

Ephraim was silent too. He looked at his son. For a moment it seemed to him that his son was about to collapse on the floor, and Ephraim was ready to hurry over to him and support him. But the boy did not fall or collapse. He continued to stand in the same place. The long hair was his mother's hair and the flush on the cheeks was also Bella-Yaffa's, but the downy beard annoyed Ephraim. But he quickly pulled himself together and his heart contracted with pity and dread.

"How are you, Na'aman?" and Ephraim himself was alarmed to hear his own voice.

The boy stretched his arms again, as if to ask forgiveness for what he had done.

This time the physician was quickly called to the room, for Na'aman refused to come out of the house with his father. The physician advised that Na'aman be taken to a hospital, and Ephraim asked if it would not be best to take him home, back to the Land of Israel.

Upon hearing this Na'aman pushed himself into a corner of the room, pressed his hands against the wall, and whispered, "I don't want to go there."

And the physician also expressed his opinion that in

the Land of Israel they would not find the specialists needed to treat the disease, and that it would be better for him to stay here, until he was better, and then he could go home if he wished.

That night Na'aman was taken to a special ward in the hospital and his father stayed beside him all night. Toward morning he heard a kind of wailing sound from his son's bed. And he bent over the boy and whispered, "Na'aman, won't you tell me, what have I done to you? Who has done this to you?"

But it appeared that Na'aman had wailed in his sleep. He did not open his eyes, and made no response.

After several days Ephraim took a train to Marseilles and there boarded a ship to return to his house and his orchards.

16.

Ephraim Abramson was forty-seven years old when he returned from his journey, and he kept his vow and never again trod outside the borders of the Land of Israel to the end of his days, forty-three years later.

Upon his return he made a report to the Citrus Growers' Association, and although it was a report of successive triumphs and achievements, the farmers wondered why he delivered it without a smile, speaking in a severe tone and having a sealed, opaque expression on his face:

an expression which stayed with him all the days of his life.

When he completed his dealings with the Association he returned to his house. He received the news about the marriage of Sarah and Aminadav in angry silence, and both youngsters were not a little surprised that he uttered no remark and found no fault with the matter. One could say that they were even a little offended. One cannot say that Aminadav stood in awe of his step-father, but it is certain that he had never been given the opportunity of exonerating himself before him, or of meeting him in quarrel and reconciliation. In these special circumstances of his marriage with Sarah, he had hoped that Ephraim would get angry, and that finally there would be reconciliation, which would allow Aminadav to find out how much Ephraim liked him. But all this came to nothing.

"Sarah will give birth in our house," Ephraim said to Rivka in their room. "But after the birth I will give them money to go to a place of their own and set up house as they see fit."

Rivka did not protest against this. She could not demand that Ephraim make himself a figure of contempt in the settlement twice on her account. For she supposed that the responsibility for Aminadav's deeds lay upon her shoulders, and what Ephraim had dared to do when he took her to wife in spite of the objections of the settlement Council was enough for her.

About a year before the World War, Sarah bore Aminadav their first son, and they called him Oved.* "We are laborers of the field," Ephraim said.

Within less than half a year Sarah and Aminadav moved to Tel Aviv with their son and there Aminadav founded a factory to make bricks and blocks, and he busied himself with it together with two workers. It was Sarah who handled the business with the contractors and builders. They took a student from the Herzliah Gymnasium into their flat in Rothschild Boulevard and in the afternoons the girl looked after Oved and the household and Sarah sat over the accounts with the builders and contractors and also did the rounds of various buildings to collect debts and receive orders for the factory.

About a year later Sarah gave birth to another son and he was called Elyakum, and several months later the World War broke out and put an end to house-building in Tel Aviv and the factory for bricks and blocks was closed.

Then came years of hunger and grief, expulsions and exile, years erased from the book of life. The orange trade ceased; also the locusts of the year 1913 had devastated many orchards and the farmers were down to a crust of bread.

About a month after the outbreak of the war Ephraim received a letter from France, among other letters of commerce and Association business, and in it there was a message that Na'aman had put an end to his life.

---

*The name in Hebrew means "laborer."

Ephraim Abramson held the letter open in his hands, reread it several times, closed his eyes and said to himself: They're both dead, then, both the mother and the son. They are writing to me here that the mother is dead too. There can be no doubt that this is what they want to tell me.

He did not tell Rivka the message from Paris, but he went to the orange grove, which had stood in full bloom only a year before but now was desolate and scorched, its branches pricking whoever approached them. He wandered among the naked trunks, waving his fist and kicking the dry clumps of earth. He emitted fragments of verses he remembered, such as "The earth is given into the hand of the wicked" and "Let the day perish wherein I was born. . . . Let that day be darkness. . . . That night, let darkness seize upon it," until he dropped onto his knees and sat on the ground, took hold of the trunk of a tree, shook it, and shouted, "Uproot, uproot it all from the roots, away to the devils and demons. . . . For what and for whom have I spent my days and spilt my blood? Whom do I have here, what do I have here? Na'aman, my son, Na'aman, my beloved, why did I let you leave your father's house? Why did I take you to those accursed lands? . . . My orphan, harp-playing youth, soft and tender sapling, I killed you, I am the murderer, I the president of the citrus growers, my heart sought after the abhorrent honor. Mad and miserable fool. Why did I refuse to believe that Bella had chosen death, preferring her death to her life with me? . . .

Requiem for Na'aman

Where were my eyes and my heart, when I saw her wandering around at home like a ghost? A house I gave her, orchards I planted for her sake . . . but she didn't want any of that. . . . She had melodies in her head and she wanted to return to those melodies. . . . Coarse beast that I am, a horse harnessed to a cart, I walked in the furrow without seeing a thing, my heart sealed like an empty barrel. . . . I needed to grasp the hand of Doctor Weizmann, . . . to wear a black suit, like one of the empty fools whom desire overtakes to go where no one knows him. . . . Who will forgive me, who will tell me I am an abominable, vile person? And you, who no longer live, my loved ones, my only ones, why should I live without you?"

Ephraim dropped down between the severed trunks, his face in the dust, until sleep fell upon him. And in his dream he was sitting at a meeting of the Citrus-Growers' Association, listening, when suddenly he remembered that the children were not covered, and might catch cold. He left the meeting hall, crossed the corridor and entered the children's room and stood in the doorway. A great happiness flooded his soul and he said to himself, Behold, a house full of all that is good, my cup runneth over, whither shall I bear my happiness?

The children's room was dark and he seemed to hear the sound of soft breathing afloat in its space. Then he remembered that he had come to cover the children. He approached the bed and found it empty. He screamed in terror and awoke from his sleep.

When he turned his face from the earth he saw sky and stars, and heard the voices of the night animals. He remembered his dream, and said to himself, "If the empty children's room were full, and the full assembly hall of the Association empty, how wonderful life could be." His face became contorted and he spat out the dirt and roots that had stuck to his mouth and teeth, spitting over and over again, and then stood up. "To the stable," he said to himself. "The horse's place is in the stable. Go and chew straw, coarse beast."

17.

THE INHABITANTS OF Tel Aviv were exiled northward by the Turks, and Sarah and Aminadav, with their two children Oved and Elyakum, arrived in a cart with a few belongings and staked a tent beside the settlement from which Ephraim's sister had come. The local people showed them the house where she had lived, where she had lost her husband and her three children.

In the settlements in the south the people hesitated and wandered about before scattering in various directions, some to the north and some to Egypt to the camp of the English. Ephraim and Rivka and young Herzl went into Egypt and dwelled there for four years.

In Egypt Ephraim happened to meet the emissaries of the Baron de Menasseh, and with their assistance found some contracting jobs in Alexandria, where he rented a small flat for his family. Rivka found work as a cook in a Jewish restaurant near the harbor.

The events of the Great War did not touch Ephraim's heart except insofar as they were connected with the Land of Israel; and everything he wanted to know about the Land of Israel he would find out from Monsieur Alex, who would occasionally arrive in Cairo, and Ephraim would travel there, to hear news, to revive his soul. And on his return from Cairo he would sit down at dinner, commanding Rivka to shut the shutters and commanding Herzl to listen and to keep the secrets to himself.

And the secrets were many and painful. A group of spies from Zichron Ya'acov served the English faithfully, because the English would be the masters of the Land of Israel when the war ended. And this group was composed purely of farmers' sons, of course, for the love of the land fills their hearts and they are ready to sacrifice their lives on the altar of the motherland. Opposed to them stood the workers from the groups and communes of various kinds, and these cleaved to their Turkish masters out of fear, terrified by the sound of a fluttering leaf and disturbing the spies in their work. There had already been a case where they had handed over one of the heroes of NILI* to his Turkish pursuers, who had sent him to execution in Constantinople.

---

*A group of Jews who during World War I worked in Palestine for Allied intelligence in the hope of ensuring future Jewish settlement. The name "NILI" is an acronym of the Hebrew phrase "*Net-*

"Remember what I say to you," Ephraim would whisper to his wife Rivka and his son Herzl, "for thereof shall a fire come forth to devour our Jewish settlement for many generations. The farmers' sons will not forgive the workers; the workers will hate the farmers' sons when they realize that they were right in the first place. Jews have a powerful memory, and what they haven't forgiven Amalek for a thousand generations, they certainly won't forgive each other after only a few years."

"Well, never mind," Rivka would say. "It will all be forgotten when the war ends. That's the way of the world."

"Woman!" Ephraim said firmly. "You are not acquainted with the character of our people. This war which now holds sway in the world is like child's play compared to the wars our Jews will fight against each other during the days of peace that will come upon us."

Rivka's arguments were stilled and Herzl listened silently, and when his father concluded his story, Herzl asked, "Father, would you like me to join the spies?"

"You sit where you are for now," Ephraim commanded him. "When you grow up and become a man there will be no lack of adventures for you. Don't worry about that."

And the Abramson family would return to their affairs waiting for the end of the war, and they would

---

zach *Israel Lo Yeshaker*," which means "The eternity of Israel will not lie," taken from I Samuel 15:29.

44

gather again from time to time to hear news, when their father returned from Cairo. And between one secret night session and the next their lives were led beside still waters, even though all around them the world was going up in flames. They lived and acted as their fathers and forefathers had lived and acted for two thousand years now: ignoring the noise and the havoc made by the Gentiles, their hearts directed toward one single center, hidden and concealed deep within the heart, and its landscapes stretched along the banks of the Jordan. From the steppes of the Ukraine, the Jordan was a long way off. From Alexandria it was not far at all.

Herzl was about seventeen when he came to Alexandria with his father and mother. He spent most of his days at college, where he quickly learned English and French, and in the evenings he would spend his time in the company of some of the sons of rich Jews. His father and mother spoiled him excessively and he dressed in the attire of the sons of the wealthy, always with money in his pocket and in good spirits.

From his friends he received the necessary instruction about city customs and he soon became their leader and mentor. The group would go to Italian prostitutes and smoke cigarettes suffused with aromatic poisons. When his mustache began to grow he did not shave it off; and on the day of his death, at the age of seventy-seven, the very same mustache adorned his upper lip.

Whilst he was still young he set himself apart with

conservative manners, such as a starched collar and cuff links which matched the color of his tie. These manners too he kept up until his dying day, a bachelor who bought love for money, so as not to owe anything to man or woman.

And because he had spent his youth in a foreign country, the aura of distant places clung to him and he took care to preserve this aura and cultivated it all the days of his life.

Ephraim expected the war to end any day, so he could return to his home and his orchards; Rivka shared his expectations, and did her work both diligently and impatiently. Only Herzl acted as if he were in no hurry to get anywhere, as if nothing had gone wrong in his life. As if he were happy with his lot, as if he had been born here, and would strike roots here forever. He was young and destined to conserve his youth for a long time, because he was conservative by nature.

In time he extricated himself from the group of Jewish youngsters in Egypt and found friends among the Italians, the Arabs, and the Greeks; and had the war not ended he might well have become assimilated into the motley population of Alexandria, from the harbor of which many found a path across the Mediterranean to travel along the roads of Europe all the days of their lives.

But the war, which had made the Abramsons flee their home, did come to an end; and the return home was self-evident to an orchard owner and farmer like Ephraim.

They thanked the emissaries of the Baron de Menasseh, they thanked the restaurant proprietor, they shook hands with the warden of the college, they paid off the Arab woman who had helped in the house, and they soon forgot all these, and Egypt was wiped off the tablets of their hearts.

From Herzl's heart Egypt was not wiped away, and it was preserved in him as in a mirror, where he who sees, sees. And as for him who does not see, it is as if there is nothing there.

18.

IN 1917 THE English armies entered Jerusalem and in 1918 the war ended, and families began seeking each other out and becoming bound together again.

When the Abramson family returned to its home Herzl was twenty-one years of age, fluent in English and French because he had been educated at a mission school.

When the Abramsons entered their ruined yard they discovered that of all the buildings that had stood there only the stable remained, and only it was fit for human habitation. They therefore set up sleeping arrangements there and stayed there for several months, until they had raised the yard from its ruins.

On the first night, and also on several nights following

it, Herzl would wake up suddenly and sit up in his bed. He was making an effort to remember the precise place where he had found Sarah and Aminadav making love, thirteen years before.

The other branch of the family—Sarah and Aminadav Ben-Zion and their children—also returned and planted themselves in Tel Aviv. From the Wagner Factory in Jaffa they ordered new machines for producing bricks and blocks, and returned to their original occupation. The English authorities did not restrict building permits, and Tel Aviv started spreading toward the east and the north, and the Ben-Zions had their hands full with work.

Oved, their elder son, became a pupil in the first year at the Herzliah Gymnasium, and Elyakum, the younger, went to the kindergarten in Yehudah Halevi Street. Once a month Grandfather Ephraim would arrive from the settlement with two baskets of fruit and vegetables, and on the eves of holidays Rivka would come with chickens, eggs, honey, and cakes. Ephraim and Rivka never came together, and only during Passover did the whole family gather to conduct the Seder together, in the new house built where the old one had stood.

Thus meetings between Herzl and his sister and her husband took place only once a year, and the spirit of coolness and politeness was upon them. It is possible that the years of separation had caused this; and it is possible that the meeting in the stable was not wiped away from their memories; and although they were now adults—and perhaps because of this—they did not find a way to wipe away the memory or to turn it into a joke about childhood days.

19.

THE FARMERS OF the settlements in the south took loans from banks in London and the branch of the Anglo-Palestine Bank in Jaffa, and started to restore life to their orchards. Those whose patience was short and whose pockets were empty mortgaged and bound over the fruit of their orchards for three or even five years ahead; but Ephraim Abramson was cautious, for he foresaw the future and understood that the price of citrus would soar higher and higher, and it would be a pity to lose so much money.

When he asked the banks to lend him money on easy and long-term credit, such as the kibbutzim were receiving, he was told by the manager, Zalman David Levontin, that the kibbutzim were receiving money from special national funds, because they were idealists and did not seek immediate profits, their sole aim being to work the land and to create a new kind of society, a society without greed for profit, without possession, without private property.

"Where did you get that from?" Ephraim was astounded.

"That's what they say," replied Mr. Levontin, the manager of the Anglo-Palestine Bank.

"And we farmers, what are we?" Ephraim raised his voice. "Did we lick honey during the days of the Turks? I, am I greedy for gain? Look at my hands, Mr. Levontin. What do they look like, a cardsharp's hands? Or what? What are these things you are saying to me?"

Mr. Levontin smiled and said to Ephraim that this was the new fashion: the farmers who had come at the end of the previous century—they were farmers, like all farmers in the world; whereas the new ones, who had come after 1905 and had established the commune Daganiah, were idealists. "And if you don't think this is right, Mr. Abramson, you're entitled to write an article in the newspaper."

This story made Ephraim's blood boil so much that he put it down as the first item on the agenda of the next meeting of the Citrus-Growers' Association. And at that meeting he summarized the dispute, and this is what he said to his colleagues:

"Whoever is satisfied with the situation, let him go back home and rest on his bed. But those whose heart is awake will attend to this new thing. What is the innovation? I'll tell you what the innovation is. A man who abhors the life of the small grocery shop, the life of a pedlar wandering from village to village, wheeling and dealing, in degradation and idleness, and comes to the Land of Israel so as to live like the rest of mankind, to care for his own family honorably, to raise children who are free, and to round out his life in his own house and in his own bed, such a man is a farmer, like all the farmers in the world, which is to say, a coarse beast, greedy for gain, and wicked. Whereas a person who has tried his hand at idolatry, at Social-Revolutionism and Bolshevikism, until the Gentiles came and kicked him in the buttocks, pardon me, Your Honors; such a man, when he comes to the Land of Israel to live without wedding canopy and ceremony, and tells us stories about how he has no need for money and no desire for property, and he is purity itself and sleekness, a creature not of this world, a seeker of the good of the entire world, on condition that he be given loans from special funds, on easy terms of credit or preferably on no terms at all; such a person is called an idealist.

"Gentlemen and fellow citrus-growers, and now, I hereby declare that such a thing as communal life does not exist at all, never existed, and was not created, but is like a fools' parable, to deceive and to despoil us of our status. To despoil us and our entire enterprise, this land, which we have worked with our sweat and our blood since the dawn of our youth. Take note: I have warned you, and it is better to be notified an hour earlier.

"And I will say one more thing to you, gentlemen, some kind of thing I have thought over in my bed at night and it gives me no rest, it's some kind of idea. I say to myself, what can one demand of a man, of flesh and blood? One can demand that he should not be a robber, that he work by the sweat of his brow, that he give charity to the poor. Such demands a man can somehow meet, although with great difficulty, gentlemen. But to come to a man and to tell him: Listen, from today on you will work, but you will get no payment. You'll sweat all day in the fields, but in the evening you won't come home to the bowl of soup such as you love, as your wife knows how to prepare for you; but you will walk like that cow to the cow shed, and there you will receive fodder, just like everyone else, given in a fixed measure on the collective dining room table; and after you have bathed your flesh in the communal shower, in the presence of naked women, pardon the expression, you won't return to your home to give your children a good-night kiss, but to the collective children's house where the nurse will allow you to be with your children for precisely one hour or one-and-a-half hours, and then you will return to your empty house, because the children have been taken by the commune into a special house. . . . I have investigated all this very thoroughly, since Levontin told me about the credit they're getting from special funds. . . . They can't tell me such fairy tales. This cannot be asked of human beings. Not for any length of time. All this will go bankrupt in a matter of a few years, ten years at the most . . . and then there also won't be anyone there to return the loans to the national funds. . . . What, anyway, are these national funds? Who gives the money? Not Jews? So what then? So nothing. One day the man in the commune will wake up and say, I abhor it. And then he will go and steal money from the communal safe. Then he will stop working and he will cheat his fellows. And his fellows will cheat him. And all of them together will cheat the people of Israel, and this entire affair will pass away from the world.

"You cannot say to a human being, Don't be a human being—be higher than that, be a saint, be righteous. . . . Too many demands such as these and what will be the outcome? The outcome will be a nation of cheats and swindlers. That is what I have been thinking these last nights, and I say to you, we have to demand from our banks the same terms the kibbutzim are getting. This is something we cannot demand from a bank in London, but we can and must demand it from Levontin. He will put it before the Zionist Executive. And we'll see what they decide. Don't give in, gentlemen!"

A few claps were heard in the room, but immediately a silence prevailed.

They have not understood, Ephraim said to himself, and he also did not mind very much. He knew how to guide his own ship in a stormy sea, and if his fellows could not sense the approaching storm, then only he who knew how to swim would save his soul.

There were some young men at the meeting who later told their friends about what Ephraim Abramson had said. The word passed from mouth to ear and reached Tel Aviv, where it rolled to the members of the Histadrut, the Hebrew Workers' Federation in the Land of Israel, and they told one of the secretaries of the kibbutzim. And when these things reached the ears of those assembled in the General Assembly of a kibbutz in the Galilee, they wore a new and remote form and this, more or less, is what was said: "As we have learned from Marx and Borochov, we know that the bourgeoisie organizes itself for counteraction whenever the proletariat takes another step on its path to liberation. We are therefore not at all surprised at the news that has arrived from the settlements in the south. There the Boazes are meeting, those Jewish kulaks,* most of whose profits come from cheap Arab labor, and they are scheming up plans to fight us. At their head stands a man named Abramowitz or Rabinowitz, and we have no cause for alarm. Within several years, ten years at the most, those kulaks will start disappearing from here. They won't last, because they have nothing to aspire to apart from money, and this they can make more of in America than here. They'll get out of here and this land will be the pioneer of the world in true socialism.

"And if I may be allowed to quote a passage from the Bible," the speaker concluded his speech, "through us will be fulfilled the words 'For out of Zion shall go forth the Law,' except that this time it will be the Law of Karl Marx, which by the way is not so far from the Law of Moses, if one knows how to read the Bible correctly."

These things happened at the beginning of the Twenties of this century. By the middle of the Twenties the Jewish population in the Land of Israel was already di-

---

*A rich Russian peasant who is a dictator in his village.

vided into two clear camps: the bourgeoisie and the socialists. All the other divisions, which after many years
formed thirty-six political factions fighting against each
other in flaming fury, outwardly, and making deals with
each other under the table, inwardly—these were nothing but tumors, like cancerous outgrowths, of those two
camps: Ephraim Abramson on the one side, and Karl
Marx on the other.

"I told you!" Ephraim reproved his fellows at one of
their meetings, twenty-five years later. But by then his
fellows no longer knew what he meant.

"What's the old man talking about?" They shrugged
their shoulders at him. "Why, his own grandson went to
a kibbutz."

But that is yet to be told, and meanwhile we are still
in the Twenties.

20.

ONE DAY IN 1921 Ephraim was making his way from his
settlement to Tel Aviv, and when he passed close to the
eastern quarters of Jaffa, among the orchards, he met
Arabs on his way, and their faces were not as in times
past. He knew in his heart that the events which were
taking place there were not good, and he turned from
his way and arrived in Tel Aviv by a circuitous route,
through the fields of Mikveh-Israel.

When he reached the house of Sarah and Aminadav,

carrying with him the two baskets of fruit and vegetables, he found the household busy trying to revive Oved.
The boy had gone to the Herzliah Gymnasium in the
morning and there he had seen people gathering and
whispering. Then a corpse was brought in, wrapped in
blankets, and it was laid down in the yard. Oved nudged
his way between the legs of the gathered people and saw
Brenner the teacher lying there stabbed, with closed
eyes, on the blanket, his beard stained with blood. He
had come home and had been vomiting all day, wailing
and not answering when spoken to.

"So, it's a pogrom," said Ephraim. "The Arabs are
trying to do to us what the Ukrainians and Russians
did."

That year the Jews in the Land of Israel started to
stock up weapons and organize themselves for self-de-
fense. The older pupils at the Gymnasium were made to
swear an oath at night on the Bible and a revolver. And
in the settlements the farmers went out on guard by
themselves and the Arab guards were dismissed from
their positions.

In 1929, when the second pogrom erupted, the six-
teen-year-old Oved was already a unit commander of the
Haganah,* and spent his nights away from home, in flats
at the end of Ha-Yarkon Street, opposite Hassan-Bek
Mosque, on the border of Jaffa. During those riots it
happened that an Arab lemon-sorbet hawker fell upon a

---

*The left-of-center underground military organization of the Jew-
ish population in Palestine.

Requiem for Na'aman

Jewish cart-driver and started to stab him with a dagger; Oved, standing at a window, aimed his revolver, shot the Arab, and killed him. When he came home in the morning, to sleep and regain some strength, he could not fall asleep. But he did not vomit and he did not wail, and when at noon his mother offered him lunch, he sat down at the table and ate, as in days gone by. His younger brother, fifteen-year-old Elyakum, was cleaning Oved's revolver and noticed that the barrel was fouled.

"Did you shoot last night?" he asked his brother in admiration.

"Do your own work and don't ask questions," Oved scolded him from his place at the table.

Obligation to secrecy was a basic principle in the Haganah. Even Sarah and Aminadav did not question their first son at all.

Oved was a quick and talented lad, and as he had entered the Gymnasium before he was six, he completed his studies before he turned eighteen, and in 1930 his parents dispatched him to Jerusalem to study at the law school.

Sarah and Aminadav now headed two factories, one for bricks and blocks, and the other for textiles. By what they saw and perceived about their two sons, it was clear to them that only Oved would be capable of continuing what his parents had begun. He was acute and practical, industrious and diligent in everything he did. Elyakum was a difficult problem. Not that he was feeble-minded, God forbid. On the contrary, he read a lot and went to the theater and to concerts, but it was getting him nowhere. At school he neglected his studies and the marks he brought home at the end of the year were dreadful and shameful. It was evident that he would never be any good at business. What was he fit for—God alone knew. Sarah drove him with a heavy hand and kept telling him that all the family's money was being wasted on tutors, whom they had to hire for him during vacations to enable him to pass exams. And Aminadav did not have free time to talk with his son Elyakum, and the son was very grateful to him for that.

Ephraim alone liked Elyakum and in secret showered him with gifts of money, so that he could buy books and records. With that same money which the grandfather put into his grandson's hands Elyakum would set out on trips around the country, disappearing from home and returning at the end of a week or two, not telling his parents a thing. Sarah would scold her father for pampering this misfit and Ephraim would reply and say, "You busy yourself with Oved, because he's a sure investment; leave Elyakum to me. He is a complete loss, and I am prepared to take a risk. Why should you care?"

Within three years Oved completed his studies in Jerusalem with great success and was crowned with a lawyer's degree. Not only that, but he also found himself a girl of the Cordoviero family, an ancient and distinguished Sephardic* family, and the girl's name was

---

*Broadly speaking, Ashkenazis are European Jews. Sephardis are Jews from North Africa and Spain.

Requiem for Na'aman

Rachel, and her parents owned much property, a resident district in Jerusalem, lands around Tiberias and also east of Tel Aviv and on Mount Canaan, and her father was a well-known lawyer, a specialist in land registry matters, and one of her uncles was a judge.

In 1934 the wedding of Oved and Rachel took place in Jerusalem, and the Ben-Zion family and the Abramson family went up to Jerusalem and stayed at the Warshawsky Hotel for three days, to celebrate the matrimonial alliance and to make the acquaintance of the Cordoviero family.

Rivka sewed herself a special dress for her grandson's wedding and Ephraim wore the suit he had taken to Europe twenty-two years earlier. An expert tailor from the settlement of Rehovot let it out in the necessary places, and after ironing the old seams were almost invisible.

Nevertheless the two of them looked somewhat like beggars, or commoners, dressed up for the day, when compared to the splendid presence of the Cordoviero family.

The distinguished Sephardic Jews of Jerusalem in no way resembled the few Sephardic Jews who were in the settlements and in Tel Aviv. Not only were their houses furnished in European taste of the nineteenth century, and there were Persian carpets, Damascus copperware, and cabinets inlaid with mother-of-pearl and silver and gold threads, but also they had an ancient, dignified appearance. It was perhaps the dignified appearance of famous and resolute rabbis, perhaps the dignified appearance of great merchants from the towns of Russia and the Caucasus in times past. But these Sephardis were not Russians, they were an exotic kind of human being, whom Ephraim suspected of being too close to the Arabs, or the Turks, or other creatures of the Orient.

The Cordovieros received the Ben-Zions and the Abramsons with lofty cordiality, but Ephraim felt that they were exaggerating their hospitality to conceal a heartfelt contempt, or a kind of pity, or perhaps even fear and suspicion; and he was in a foul mood during all three days of their stay in Jerusalem.

According to the standing of the household and according to what people said, Ephraim had no ground for regretting the match. Especially as he had no worries, God forbid, about Oved's fate. The lad was like that cat which, if he fell, would land on all fours and not get hurt. And yet Ephraim felt that his grandson was going beyond the grasp of the family and that, one might even say, he was going beyond the grasp of the tribe, the tribe of the Abramsons from Russia, farming pioneers of the Land of Israel.

"Never mind," he said to Rivka, after the couple had come out from under the canopy, properly married, true, but nevertheless married by a Sephardic rabbi, in a black robe and with a black turban on his head, who had chanted nuptial chants such as Ephraim's forefathers had never known. "Never mind, let it be a good omen and good fortune. Oved will find his way even beyond the remote, Dark Mountains, all the more so among those Jews, who in the end are no less Jews than we are. . . . As for me, I am worried about Elyakum, not about Oved."

He prophesied and did not know what he prophesied.

Whilst the guests were still congratulating the couple and turning toward the tables laid out with all manner of good things, Elyakum was enjoying the company of some youths from among the dignitaries of Jerusalem, Sephardis and Ashkenazis, who had been invited to the wedding, some on the strength of family relationships and some on the strength of the legal profession or the land trade. And there were also some Arab guests there, from the most venerable families in Jerusalem. And in that company, when the wine had been poured and the glasses had been clinked against each other, and the guests had already become heady, Elyakum was carried away in his speech and talked effusively and said: "I have a question to ask, and I want to understand . . . simply because there's one thing I don't understand: where are you headed, all of you here? Look here, my brother has already become a lawyer, and all of you too . . . what are you? Merchants, speculators, money-rakers, or what? Where does all this lead to? In other words: what for? And aren't we dealing here with the Land of Israel . . . that means a dream. Or how shall we say it? An ideal. . . . Want to put right something that has been flawed, to change, to remedy a kind of defect, or, let's say, to remedy a disease. . . . Yes, a Jewish disease, but also a world disease. . . . I will say it clearly, without any circumlocutions. . . . Shall we say it like this: we've returned here after two thousand years, so why the hell did we go to all this bother in the first place to come here? That is the question. Why are people killed and dying here? What did we have all this for? And I say: To realize a dream . . . a dream. So what did we dream, then? We dreamed a beautiful world, beautiful human beings, a kind of purity, a different kind of joy, new, not to be found in exile. . . . And here, what? Lawyers, banks, cheap labor, exploiting the Arabs, licking the asses of the English and receiving all kinds of jobs. . . . What is it? It's filth. For this it's not worth it, gentlemen. . . . Think for yourselves and answer me: was it worth it to come to swamps and malaria and murders, in order to be lawyers and to work in a bank? . . . Look to the window, gentlemen, and you will see what a splendid light glows upon Jerusalem, how the stones burn, gentlemen. . . . Here there's a wonderful fire, go out into it and get burned in it, purified in that fire, gentlemen; this is an opportunity that comes to our people once in a thousand years, once in two thousand, in fact. . . . So what then? Lawyers, clerks of the court, clerks, petty speculators, ha? That's it? I ask, why all of a sudden?"

His voice soared higher and higher and all the guests heard the ends of his statements and some of them were astounded, whilst others chuckled and wondered and asked each other: Who's the joker? And when the wedding guests learned that he was the bridegroom's brother they were dumbfounded, because Oved had indeed made a good impression.

And the Arab guests were told that the bridegroom's brother had made a speech blessing the marriage.

Only Ephraim, who had listened closely to his grandson's speech, smiled to himself, and leaned over to Rivka and whispered in her ear, "He has inherited the gift of speech-making from me. Only it's a pity he didn't inherit a few other qualities too. If he were to say these things after he already had an orchard or a factory, never mind. It would even be good. But like this, penniless and barefoot? I knew that this child had to be looked after. I knew in my heart. I know several Abramsons who aren't exactly Abramsons. We'll have to take the lad in hand."

Those gathered there behaved toward Elyakum and his speech the way people behave toward a man overcome by wine. They laughed, some of them even applauded, and all returned to what was offered to them on the tables.

Oved was annoyed, but Rachel calmed him down and said that, on the contrary, his brother was very nice. He spoke well and did not suffer from stage fright. It was a pity he had not studied law. Sarah and Aminadav rushed in alarm to their younger son and took him to a side room, where Aminadav told him that if he wasn't capable of holding a drink, he should at least hold his tongue and not disgrace himself on a day like this and at a moment like this.

"Father," Elyakum said to him, "I have something more to tell you, and this time in private. Listen well: in a week's time I'm going to a kibbutz. It has been decided. And don't get angry. I also have a pleasant surprise for you, for you and for my brother the lawyer. I am renouncing my share of the inheritance. I have no need for money or a factory. How do you like that?"

"We're not going to die so soon," his mother Sarah said to him, "and stop prattling on about inheritances. No one here is leaving you any inheritance as yet. As for this kibbutz of yours, we'll talk about it at home. Now button up your shirt and sit down at the table like a civilized human being."

"Yes, Mother," Elyakum chuckled at her. "At your command, sir!"

He saluted to his mother and marched stiffly to the reception room, and when he appeared there some of the guests applauded him again, to the chagrin of his mother and father.

A week later Elyakum took his books and his records and left home, and a few days later his parents received a card, in which Elyakum invited them to come and visit him at his kibbutz.

From the letter they learned that he had gone to a kibbutz not far away, somewhere between Tel Aviv and the settlement where his grandfather lived. It appeared that Ephraim had not been a spendthrift, and the money he had given his grandson had not been enough for long voyages; otherwise on his trips—when he used to disap-

pear from home for a week or two—Elyakum would
surely have reached the Galilee and would have pitched
his tent there. Well, at least this was to the good. A crazy
whim, destined to pass, like every summer storm, and
Elyakum was not so much of a fool as to exchange his
parents' home for a kibbutz. Tomorrow, or in a matter
of days, he would come back home, and his mother
would wipe his nose for him.

21.

ELYAKUM DID NOT return to his parents' home, not after
a day, not after two days, and not after a year or two.

When he arrived at the kibbutz he received a tent of
his own, in the quarter of the bachelors who were can-
didates for membership in the kibbutz. The next day he
was given a cart drawn by two mules, which he loaded
with manure in the cow sheds and drove out to the vegetable allotments and to the fields. In the evenings, when
he returned from the shower, he would go to the dining
room and from there to his tent, to read a book or to
listen to music on the gramophone he had brought with
him. And in the mornings—the same thing over again:
a first breakfast at five o'clock in the dining room, the
ride to the cow sheds, a second breakfast in the field, and
a long work day, all of it free for thinking and soul-
searching.

Twice a week he would go to the room of Meshulam

Ha-Gelili, who was a kind of eternal youth, according to his blue eyes and his pink cheeks, and quite an elderly man, according to his age and his bald pate. There Elyakum would read what the man had written between one meeting and the next. This man was working assiduously on preparing a program, from which members of all the kibbutzim would be able to recognize what their aspirations were and how to behave according to principles set for them by Meshulam Ha-Gelili. After Elyakum had studied the papers, they would clarify the difficult corpora of issues and go on arguing extensively until the morning light. And in the morning Meshulam Ha-Gelili would go off to sleep in his bed and Elyakum would go off to collect his manure. He had not yet found a common language with the other people in the kibbutz.

On Saturdays he would take one of his mules and ride out to the fields, so that he could think undisturbed. But the mule is not a riding animal and rebels against its rider, and so it happened that Elyakum's mule went wild and burst into a crazy gallop, leaping up on its hind legs and kicking at the air, until it threw its rider to the ground, and before running off into the fields gave him a kick in the ribs. Elyakum did not get up from that fall until after a week's time, during which he lay in bed, finding it very difficult to breathe, as one of his ribs was cracked.

When the matter was discussed at the kibbutz meeting, there were members who said, with reservations, that a city youth, accustomed to city pleasures, should not ride mules. Other members remarked that the animals too were entitled to a day of rest, and this was even written in the Torah, and Elyakum should be explicitly forbidden to exploit the mules. But there were also members who defended Elyakum, and who told those present at the meeting that in the journal *Ha-Poel Ha-Tzair*, "The Young Worker," they had seen an article by Elyakum on Yosef Chaim Brenner.*

"Of course, it is difficult to demand a sense of responsibility from such a character," said those who came to Elyakum's defense.

On this Meshulam Ha-Gelili remarked, "On the contrary, precisely because he wields a pen, and also carries the burden of work in the fields, one must see in him the embodiment of the new man."

The members did not understand exactly what he meant, and Meshulam Ha-Gelili did not explain, and no one asked him to explain, because if he opened his mouth he would be liable to go on talking until the morning light and it would be a waste of energy.

Elyakum accepted the verdict, and from then on he would go out to the fields on Saturdays on foot, and finally found that it was better that way. Walking is fine for thinking, and riding is a wild thing; and apart from that they were right, those who said that an animal also has the right to rest.

---

*A famous writer (1880–1921) who came from Russia to the Land of Israel.

Benjamin Tammuz

The case of the rights and the duties in kibbutz society was one of the difficult corpora of issues Meshulam Ha-Gelili dealt with in his essay. He claimed, for example, that manual labor is a great privilege, of which not everyone is worthy; first of all a man has to prove himself, and as long as he has not proved himself or prepared himself from within, it is doubtful whether he is worthy of playing a part in the social symphony. Thus he wrote explicitly, and Elyakum was delighted with the musical metaphor and saw it as a hint at the benefit of music and at the essence of its legitimacy in kibbutz society.

Having found a liking for music in Meshulam Ha-Gelili's writings, he invited him one evening to his tent, to hear some records. Meshulam had no family obligations, having separated from his wife (the second one), and he visited his children in the afternoon hours, on the lawn of the children's house, according to the fixed rule, two hours each day, before supper. So Meshulam came to Elyakum's tent, took one look at the gramophone, and said, "You'd best put that thing in the culture room, so that all the members can hear the music. And in the meantime let's see what you have. Put on a good record."

Elyakum was alarmed. "In the culture room? But there they read newspapers and converse. It's impossible to listen to music there."

"And how do you expect to accustom our members to more refined pleasures, if you don't try? And apart from that, in principle, you have no right to keep property, an instrument or a machine, beyond the reach of the other members. . . . That is, the budget doesn't suffice. . . . But in the meantime, let's see what you have. Put on something good."

Elyakum put a record on the turntable, Bach's "Toccata and Fugue," conducted by Stokowski, and started to turn the handle. "I'll tell you, Meshulam," he said, thinking aloud, "if you have already decided I haven't the right, perhaps it is worthwhile to ask the members. Perhaps they don't even want it in the culture room."

And when the first notes burst from the cabinet, Meshulam's face became contorted and he called out in alarm, "Stop that. . . . Don't you have something popular, some songs or folk dances?"

Elyakum said he did not, and almost breathed in relief, but Meshulam said that good records could be bought from the budget for culture, it was not so expensive. The main thing was the gramophone itself, and he would bring the matter before the assembly.

And then they launched themselves into a discussion of programmatic topics, but that same night Elyakum did not comprehend much of the ideas, and his heart foretold difficulties for him.

Several months later—with the gramophone still in his tent, for Meshulam Ha-Gelili was a forgetful and absentminded man, wholly given to the nuclei of his general ideas—the first group of boys and girls from Germany arrived in the kibbutz. Their parents had remained in Berlin, in Frankfurt and in the other places, in order to save what they could from the Nazis who had come to power, but they made their sons and daughters flee to the Land of Israel, so that they might join them later on. And among the arrivals there was a girl, named Liesl, and she had brought a violin with her. And from the moment Elyakum saw the violin he started day-dreaming. He comes back from the field, showers, and turns toward the dining room, and there Liesl sits at the table and keeps a place for him near her, and he comes and sits next to her, makes a salad with his own hands, and pours her soup out with a ladle. And when she drinks the soup he whispers in her ear and asks her how far she has already reached in playing the violin, and she smiles and does not divulge a thing to him. But when they come to his tent she takes the violin out of its case and, as if thunderstruck, he listens to a chaconne by Bach. All night long he listens to her playing and toward morning he caresses her hair and she promises him to return each and every night.

Elyakum followed Liesl with his eyes for many weeks, and evening after evening he would see her in the dining room, sitting among the boys and girls who had come from Germany. After the meal she would get up and depart with them to the house where they lived, next to the school. One time it was Liesl's turn in the kitchen and another time she served and brought the tureens of soup around to the tables. When she placed the tureen on his table, Elyakum said thank you to her. She looked at him in astonishment and continued with her work. That night a decision ripened in his heart, but it took him another week to put his decision into practice, because in the meantime he had a cold. And verily a week later he hastily finished his supper and went out to stand on guard by the exit door. Soon he saw Liesl coming out, talking with a girlfriend. Elyakum marched straight like a soldier breaking ranks, and slightly startled the two girls. He did not go back on his decision and said to Liesl, "I would like to speak with you, if possible."

"With me alone?" asked Liesl. "Or can my girlfriend also come?"

"With you alone," said Elyakum.

"Excuse me," said Liesl to her girlfriend, who immediately continued on her way. "Where are we talking?"

Although Elyakum was amazed and delighted at the enormity of his success, he could not but wonder at the ease with which the fortress had been captured. Almost immediately he began to have grave doubts about the moral quality of the German youth, but he was not free to consider the subject seriously, because Liesl immediately went on and asked, "Do you want to walk a bit over there?"

She pointed toward the road that led to the orchards.

When he found himself walking beside her down the slope of the hill, Liesl was chattering without restraint and said, "You're odd people in the Land of Israel. . . . Or is it only in the kibbutzim? I don't know yet Tel Aviv. . . . But in the kibbutz it's very odd. The young people are terribly shy, or they are afraid of us, because we came from Europe, I don't know. . . . They don't approach us and they don't make any contact. However the old ones are devils out of hell, wandering hands, ready for all sorts of adventures; real Don Juans, professionals. . . . How do you explain that?"

Elyakum first wanted to know if she had noticed him before this. "I'm the one who thanked you when you served in the dining room," he said to her.

"I don't remember," said Liesl. "I've made the acquaintance of so many people lately; it blurs you, you know. . . . So what do you say about the fact that the lads like you are shy and the old men frisk about like youths. . . . Is that not strange?"

"I wanted to ask you a question," said Elyakum. "That violin . . . have you been playing long?"

"Playing? What playing all of a sudden? The violin is not mine at all. That is, it belongs to the family. I was told that it is very valuable, and if I won't be able to stay in the kibbutz, then I'll sell the violin and try to manage in town. The violin, that is my capital. Why do you ask about the violin? I thought you were interested in me, or am I mistaken?"

By now Elyakum should have known that he had made a mistaken bargain, but he missed the opportunity. The night was cool and full of voices of crickets and night fowl, and Liesl asked a simple and understandable question: "Do I please you? Tell me, don't be afraid."

And to enable him to consider the question and also to give him matter with which to weigh his answer, Liesl grasped his head and kissed him on the mouth.

"Is that to your taste?" she urged him, and it seemed to him that she was about to take offense.

Requiem for Na'aman

"Decidedly," he said. "I don't rule out the possibility of such relationships also; it's decidedly natural . . . if there is a spiritual relationship between two human beings, naturally. . . . You are very beautiful, I think."

"And what relationship is there now between the human beings? Show some appreciation, so that I will understand what you're blabbering about."

And now she resumed and embraced him by the shoulders and kissed him again on the mouth.

Elyakum's entire body started to tremble.

"Is that how you are?" she said and with her right hand circled his waist, pressing him to her. "You're like all the other youths in this place. . . . A strange bunch. . . . I think it would be better if we sat here a bit, on this stone. . . . Here, like this. You put your head on me, don't be afraid."

Elyakum lay on his back, his head on her knees, and saw a greenish half-moon. His nostrils filled with the smell of irrigated soil and on the other side of the orchard, where the well house was, someone was trying vainly to start the motor.

"It won't start," said Liesl. "Just like you."

Elyakum got up and sat on the ground opposite her. Beside them continued the road leading into the orchard and on it there were ruts from the wheels of a tractor, clods of earth which the moon endowed with the figures of small, still animals. A black snake crawled lazily across the road.

"Did you see that?" Elyakum pointed at the snake.

73

Liesl jumped up and embraced him tightly. Elyakum stroked her hair and kissed her on the temple. "Don't be afraid," he said, "it's not a poisonous snake. It is beneficial to agriculture. It eats field mice. . . . You're so soft and warm, Liesl. I feel so good being with you now."

"But I'm not beneficial to agriculture," said Liesl.

"You needn't mock me," said Elyakum. "We'll gradually become friends and get used to each other."

"Am I so loathsome that you have to get used to me gradually? Never heard of love at first sight?"

"Liesl, this isn't love at first sight. . . . You're other than me, you're completely different, your ideas are different. . . ."

"You will be surprised to see how similar we all are, silly boy. You know what? You want to return to the kibbutz?"

Elyakum grasped her tightly and she let out a short cry, playfully.

"You're not as weak as you pretend to be, child. You have the hands of a murderer. You almost dismantled me, you know. You're almost dangerous, if you want to be. So, what now: aren't we returning to the kibbutz?"

"We're not returning, Liesl, we're sitting here. And this time we'll just sit, and now I am kissing you and you be a good girl and close your eyes and I'll keep on kissing you, and I'll tell you . . . listen, I'll tell you the names of all the plants, all the wild plants that are here around us . . . and I'll describe what's happening around here . . . how the moonlight casts a spell on all the little

74

things on the earth, and how they start coming alive and moving . . . and I will explain to you why I feel so good here now with you, and also why everything is so sad, at the very same time. . . . What wonderful magic and so many things filling the heart, Liesl . . ."

She took his hand and guided it to the opening of her shirt, to her breasts. Elyakum did not resist, but continued where he had left off: "You close your eyes and I will tell you everything there is to be told. You have to listen, Liesl, because if you don't know what I have to say, we shall never get close to each other. We have to break the strangeness. . . . We met for the first time only today. . . ."

"And you're already holding my breasts for me," said Liesl.

"I'm not holding your breasts," Elyakum raised his voice, scolding. "I am stroking your breasts, and my soul is almost flying with joy."

"Thank God that you're cheerful at last. Earlier you said that with you everything is so sad."

"And so, you hear, you listen to me. That's good, it is a good omen. . . . Now I will tell you something more. I wasn't born in the kibbutz. I was born in the city, and I grew up in a bourgeois household, and my brother is a lawyer. It is very hard for me here, but I have decided to go another way, and I will not renounce it. I have a dream. . . . Do you have a dream too, Liesl?"

"I don't dream any more than I am allowed to, child. I am here alone, in a foreign country. What can I dream already? Perhaps about that one day that I'll come out of this kibbutz and find a place where there are fewer madmen. . . . Tell me, you, for example, would you agree to run away from the kibbutz with me? You have rich parents, and a brother who is a lawyer, so let them help you . . . and I can always sell the violin, if it will be worthwhile . . ."

"I gave up my inheritance and told my brother what I think of him and his profession. Liesl, you and I, two different worlds, you should know that. . . . What an awful distance there is between us, Liesl; you have no idea . . . like two different sides of the globe."

"Idiot," said Liesl. "What an idiot you are."

From that day on Elyakum and Liesl would meet almost every evening, but instead of walking along the path leading to the orchards they would go directly from the dining room to his tent. Liesl did not mind it that he put records on the gramophone, and would congratulate herself on the fact that from night to night he would forget more often to change the record and sometimes the gramophone would be silent for a whole hour.

One night she said to him, "If you have already decided to stay here, why don't you have a single friend in the kibbutz? And why didn't you have a girlfriend before I came? What kind of life do you live?"

"You know that I have a friend," Elyakum said apologetically.

"Is that a friend, that old man? He could be your father."

"Indeed he is my spiritual father, in a certain sense," said Elyakum.

"Listen, you have a father in Tel Aviv, and if you want to, you can see him within an hour. Only it is precisely to him that you don't go. . . . If I had a father in Tel Aviv, Elyakum, if I had a father, I wouldn't rot here for another moment. . . . And you blabber to me about the lunatic Meshulam. . . . A father? An old lecher, not a father!"

"What a way to talk, Liesl!"

"What a way to talk? I will tell you. I am telling you simple things. That spiritual father of yours has been divorced twice, and now he's getting all his girlfriends pregnant, one after the other; and then he sends them to the Histadrut Trade Union Health Service in Tel Aviv to have an abortion . . . that great ideologue of yours. . . . He writes them covering letters to the Histadrut Trade Union Health Service on kibbutz stationery. . . . He's a great man, Meshulam Ha-Gelili."

"There's no need to interfere in intimate matters between man and woman," Elyakum pronounced.

"Why? Doesn't what is between man and woman belong to your idealistic life? Only agriculture belongs to it?"

"Your question is a valid one, but you are looking at it from the point of view of a petty bourgeois."

"I? Petty bourgeois? Well, truly, child, can you hear what you are jabbering? Sometimes it seems to me that indeed you are an idiot."

In order to change her opinion of Meshulam Ha-Gelili, Elyakum suggested that one evening they sit and talk with him, so that she could get to know him better. Liesl laughed but agreed, and one evening the two of them entered Meshulam's room and sat down to drink coffee. Meshulam told Liesl about the circumstances in which Hitler had risen to power, and counted one by one the reasons for the disintegration of the German Social-Democracy. Then he extended his account to the anti-Semitism of the Nazis, quoted by heart from Hitler's *Mein Kampf*, and proved from signs and omens that his days of power were numbered. "But for the harm he has brought upon the Jews," and Meshulam raised his voice and threatened with his finger, "he will pay dearly. Here, you, Liesl, for example, you're a perfect victim. That villain will be trodden upon and annihilated, but who will return to you the years in which you were robbed of your family? These precious years in which you are without a father or a mother? Even though we here in the kibbutz are doing everything we can to give you a true home, a warm home, is there a substitute for father and mother? And they themselves, your parents —aren't their hearts broken, now, at this very moment whilst we're sitting here and mentioning them? He will pay dearly for the destruction he has wrought upon your young souls."

Elyakum looked at Liesl, worried that she might open her mouth and start talking about the pregnancies and the abortions. But she kept silent.

"I hope, and even somewhat believe," Meshulam Ha-

Gelili added, excitedly, "that the kibbutz society is compensating you, at least a little, for the home and the family of which you have been robbed. We, on our part, are doing all we can, and no sacrifice is hard for us. But what power do we have? Very little, and the objectives are heavier than we can bear. Forgive us, Liesl, if what is available is not always in accordance with what is desired."

"I have no complaints," said Liesl.

"You're fortunate," Meshulam smiled, "in having a friend like Elyakum."

"Elyakum is a child," said Liesl. "He's a good boy. But he's a little orphan, just like me. Orphans can cry together, but they can't help each other."

Meshulam and Elyakum left this comment without a reaction and they sipped from their cups of coffee.

After this Meshulam spoke about his life, about his struggles in the kibbutz and outside it, about his two marriages which had not turned out well, twice did not turn out well, and always for the very same reason: a lack of true affinity between the two.

"True affinity in marital life," explained Meshulam, "is a personal matter, not a social one. Since from an ideological point of view I cannot say a thing against either of my two former companions. Both are socially conscious members of the kibbutz, to this very day, and with both I can maintain crystallized ideological contact, with considerable mental satisfaction. But from the dialectical aspect there is no contradiction between this assertion and the aforementioned assertion about the lack of affinity. Mutual relations between the two genders is a sexual function, not only a social function; and here, to my sorrow, lies hidden the difficulty."

He spoke and did not elaborate, as was his way sometimes.

This time Elyakum and Liesl sipped at their coffee whilst Meshulam Ha-Gelili closed his eyes and mused to himself. And from the place where he had stopped in his musings, he said, "Sometimes I wonder if Schopenhauer did not set it out aptly concerning the corpus of marriage when he said that a man should marry twice in his lifetime: once when he is eighteen years old and she is forty years old; and once when he is forty years old and she is eighteen years old. The first time she bestows motherhood on the man. The second time the man bestows fatherhood on the woman. And also experience, in both cases. . . . And here am I, twice I married a woman of my own age. Is it any wonder that I failed?"

"Ha!" Liesl exclaimed, out of joy. "It is a great idea, but difficult. The first time he buries her, and the second time she buries him. It's a very bothersome system. Two funerals, two weddings, lawyers, rabbis. I'm for economizing. Experiments can be conducted in the laboratory. Afterward one can also marry, if it is a necessity."

"Laboratory?" Meshulam perked up his ears. The word was very ready on his lips, and he wanted to know what kind of laboratory Liesl was talking about.

"Bed," said Liesl. "A simple bed, or a double bed, for those who like comfort."

"Ah," said Meshulam. "Well, yes . . . and I was thinking that you had some kind of idea."

"Isn't that an idea?" Liesl insisted.

Elyakum was thinking that he had taken the trouble in vain to make these two meet. Liesl came from an entirely different world and only education in depth, what is called engineering of the soul, perhaps would make those changes come about.

And verily changes did come about in her, but this happened after some time. Meanwhile a year had passed since Elyakum arrived in the kibbutz. At the general meeting it was decided, with reservation, to accept him as a member with full rights and obligations. Elyakum wrote his grandfather about it, and Ephraim—who had not noticed that an entire year had passed since his grandson had gone mad—hurried in a car one Saturday to reach the hill. With his cane he stepped onto the lawn and commanded the people lying about there to be good enough to tell him where he could find Mr. Elyakum Ben-Zion.

Elyakum was summoned from his tent. He came out with Liesl to greet his grandfather.

"Who's this?" said Ephraim, pointing his cane in alarm at the bare-shinned girl with her short pants and her impudent face, who looked at him with undisguised pleasure.

"This is Liesl," said Elyakum. He embraced Ephraim by the shoulders and kissed him on his cheeks. "Come, Grandfather, we'll drink tea in the dining room. Why didn't you let me know you were coming?"

"What for? Do I need to receive permission from your executive to come here? Does not all this," and he waved his cane toward the farm buildings and twisted up his face, as if he were looking at a leper colony, "all this property come from the pocket of the private citizen? We pay taxes and they make all kinds of speculation. . . . The egg is teaching the hen how to run the chicken coop. . . . Well, come, let's go and have tea. For that tea I have already paid enough taxes."

"You have a great grandfather," Liesl whispered to Elyakum. "Don't let him leave here. I'm dying to hear him talk. What a male!"

"I told you!" replied Elyakum proudly.

"What did you tell me?" she scoffed at him. "You told me that you have a family of bourgeois, who exploit cheap Arab labor. . . . You said that your grandfather is a fossil of the older generation, who ought to be forgotten. . . . You are an idiot, Elyakum."

"What is she whispering to you over there?" Ephraim wanted to know. "Young lady, I have forgotten your name, you may speak out loud. Elyakum has no secrets from me."

"They call me Liesl," she said.

"A fine name you have chosen. Aren't there any Jewish names in the world? And what are you whispering to him? Don't be afraid of me. I am already sixty-nine."

"You're younger and nicer, sir, than this whole kibbutz," said Liesl.

"Do you hear that?" Ephraim roared in Elyakum's ear.

"Look here, your girlfriend is telling you that it is necessary to get out of here, before you become like one of
them. Elyakum, just say the word and I will buy you a
fine farm. . . . Where's the tea you mentioned? Do you
hear me? A farm with a young citrus orchard and a
house, and you will be a man, worthy of your family.
. . . That is why I came, to tell you that."

"He doesn't have a single friend here." Liesl told on
him without shame. "Apart from me, he hardly speaks
with anyone."

"That's very good," said Ephraim. "About what and
with whom can you speak here? You must pack your
suitcase and run from here, quickly. There's a large and
beautiful world outside. Both of you come and visit me
once, in the settlement. You can compel him to do it,
Miss Liesl. Women can do that, ho, ho, and how they
can."

After they had given Ephraim several glasses of tea to
drink Elyakum offered to show Ephraim around the
farm.

"I have nothing to learn from them," said Ephraim
and did not move from his place. "If they want to learn
agriculture, let them come and work with us. There is
much work, thank God, but they are lazy and they only
know to demand ever more money. Elyakum, listen, if
you don't like agriculture, perhaps something in industry
or commerce? It is no shame. We all build the land, each
in his own way. What do you think, son, tell me: you
need not be ashamed before me. And your grandmother

too asked me to pass it on to you that she is ready to give of her property. . . . You're not an orphan, Elyakum. We don't lack a thing, just a little satisfaction from you. . . . You have gone completely mad . . . to come to such a place. . . . Is this tea, this? The water your grandmother does the dishes in is better, pardon me, than this mud, phoo. . . . Listen, Miss, talk to him. You have seen the world, tell him. Where in the world has a kibbutz been heard of, except in Russia, where they are not only insane but explicitly Bolsheviks. . . . What do you say, Eli? I ask you and you don't say a word. Did they cut off your tongue?"

"Grandfather," Elyakum smiled, enjoying the sight of Liesl delighting in the speech, "I am how I am, and I love you and that's the main thing. You're a great man, but you come from a different world. . . ."

"Now you say he's a great man," Liesl interrupted him, "but you always told me that your family are exploiters and rotten bourgeois. So how is it that all of a sudden he becomes a great man? Although I agree that he's a great man and I wish he were my grandfather and not yours. . . . But why did you change your mind all of a sudden?"

"What?" Ephraim burst out. "The boy said that I am an exploiter and a bourgeois? Elyakum, tell me that to my face. Now stand up and say it, I want to hear it!"

"Grandfather," said Elyakum in alarm, "I meant it in a general sense, in terms of origin, class, world outlook . . . not personally . . ."

"I'm an exploiter?" Ephraim's wrath continued to increase. "After fifty years in the Land of Israel my mad grandson tells me I'm a parasite? What have I been doing here for fifty years? Playing cards? Ha? Tell me, you, clever by half; you have all gone completely insane. . . . The Bolsheviks have bewitched you and what you need now is a physician for madness, nothing else would be of any use. Not a thing. . . ."

Ephraim looked at his cane, as if only in it was it possible to find counsel in such a time of crisis and, almost whispering, said, "Bella, Bella, how I envy you, you knew to get out of here before all this happened; now I remain alone."

"Bella? That was your first wife, wasn't it, Grandfather?" asked Elyakum, because he was not sure and also because he wanted Liesl to understand what was being talked about. Ephraim raised his eyes from the cane and looked at the two of them as if seeing them for the first time.

"This young lady," he said to Elyakum, "what is she to you? Your girlfriend? Your bride-to-be? And if she is your bride-to-be, what are you waiting for? At least get married. Well, come on, let's see these palaces of yours. Let's see what you've managed to get done at public expense."

After they had roamed among the farm buildings, where Ephraim wanted to know how much each of the agricultural branches brought in, they did not return to what they had been talking about in the dining room.

And when they parted, Ephraim embraced Elyakum for a long while and his eyes shed small drops of tears, trickling tears. Finally he reached out a hand to Liesl, but she was not content with it, and rushed to him with an enthusiastic embrace and kissed him on his face again and again.

"I love you," she said. "I want you to come here much."

"You see?" said Ephraim to Elyakum, and turned and walked to the road.

"Idiot," said Liesl to Elyakum, "how much of an idiot you are, you really have no idea."

Soon after Ephraim's visit to the kibbutz Liesl received a letter from a relative who had settled in Nahariyah, which is in the Galilee.

"They've invited me to their settlement," said Liesl to Elyakum, "and I'm going. I don't know for how long, Elyakum, and you needn't feel offended. If I don't manage there I'll come back to you, don't worry. A girl like me is not a terrible loss, you'll always be able to find something better."

Elyakum was shocked. He immediately offered to enter in a marriage covenant with her; and when she refused he asked if the life in a kibbutz held her back from being married to him.

"Not the kibbutz," she said. "But you. You are a child, don't you understand that you are a child?"

"I am three-and-a-half years older than you," said

Elyakum. Liesl tried to laugh and stroke his face, but when she found she could not, she placed her head on his chest and started sobbing quietly.

In summer Liesl went and in autumn she returned to the kibbutz and brought her suitcase to Elyakum's tent. When he returned from the fields he found her asleep on his bed.

That evening there was a concert in the dining room. A short fellow with a huge nose and a thick and fleshy mouth played upon the violin. He had come from Jerusalem, and was going around the kibbutzim and playing. From the notice board Elyakum learned that his name was Amadeus Bieberkraut. Liesl told him that in Germany the Bieberkraut family was known as a family of musicians and also madmen. At the concert Elyakum and Liesl sat embracing, stroking each other and listening to the music. Before the end of the evening Liesl fell asleep on his shoulder, and he was compelled to wake her when all the other members got up from their seats.

"Where's that violinist?" she asked, when she opened her eyes. "Get hold of him and tell him to come over to our place. I want him to try my violin and tell me if it really is so valuable."

Elyakum obeyed and Amadeus Bieberkraut was delighted at the invitation and asked them to bring a thermos of coffee to the tent, because he could not live without coffee.

"Without preamble, gentlemen, let me tell you at once," began Bieberkraut and said, when he had entered the tent and laid his violin case down on the floor, "that I am homosexual. If that frightens you, say so now and I will buzz off."

"Does it frighten you?" Liesl asked Elyakum. "Not me."

Amadeus drank some coffee and said, "Generally in the kibbutzim I play Sarasate and Vivaldi, but in your kibbutz I feel like at home and therefore I played things that I truly love. I played for your young boys and with them made a primeval contact which may have no continuation but is important for its own sake. I am speaking about the world of ideas and not about the earthly patterns."

He tried out Liesl's violin and began jumping about in the room out of excitement. Immediately he brought a lighted match up to the opening of the violin, to see what was written inside, but he found no inscription and almost singed the strings.

"Unbelievable," he cried out in amazement. "Absolutely unbelievable."

Liesl was satisfied and soon hinted to Elyakum to get the musician out of the tent because she was tired and wanted to sleep. But Amadeus Bieberkraut sipped from his cup of coffee and sat down to work. First he played an aria by Bach on the G-string and from there he moved on, without warning, to the overture to Mendelssohn's violin concerto.

"How will this end?" Liesl whispered to Elyakum, "he comes from a family of madmen."

"I see you both like music," said Amadeus Bieber-kraut. "Well, then, I shall tell you a little about myself. . . . Might I have another cup of coffee? Playing is only one aspect of my personality, and among friends one can be candid. . . . Astrology is the core of my life, and this is in spite of what you may have heard or read in the papers. . . . There is no value in the view of the mob. And not only the mob. I will not hide from you that I have received a postcard from Albert Einstein. . . . I offered to read his horoscope for him, and he refuses. Here, the postcard is here, please, look what he writes."

Liesl and Elyakum leaned over the postcard that Amadeus Bieberkraut had drawn from a pocket of his waistcoat. In small handwriting, clear and polished, it was written:

> *Ich habe nicht gerne*
> *Wenn man schwindelt mit Sterne**
> ALBERT EINSTEIN

"Einstein's greatness I do not deny," said Amadeus, "but not with respect to astrology. Thomas Mann relates to the matter in a completely different way. . . . Here, please."

And he drew out a long letter, which stretched over several pages. Liesl looked it over.

"But he talks about homosexuality, not about astrology," she said.

---

*"I do not like it when one swindles with stars."

"In this particular letter, yes," said Amadeus. "But I have more letters, but those I have already sold to the National Library in Jerusalem. . . . This is for my livelihood, because often I don't have any money, even though my expenses are small, as I live in a cave and I don't pay rent; in spite of all that I still have expenses, especially as I must pay the boys, because they love money. . . . Here, I have a letter with me from Sigmund Freud, and that is a totally different style. He wants to buy my diary from me and I'm now preparing a fair copy for him."

"You excuse me," said Liesl. "I am very tired, and I want to sleep."

"Please do," said Amadeus. "You go to sleep and I will sit here with Elyakum and we will talk in whispers and we won't disturb you."

Liesl stretched out on the bed and fell asleep and Elyakum went to get another thermos full of coffee from the dining room.

"Among men," said Amadeus, "it's a lot simpler. . . . Here, now we will be able to talk without disturbance, and you won't regret it. I have something very important to say, something general which at the same time affects every person in this country, in kibbutzim, in Jerusalem, and in Tel Aviv. It is a prophecy, and I want you to know it. It is a night prophecy, a kind of vision confined to our land and our people. . . . It opens with an *allegro*. Here, like this: the land is green, in winter the rains water it, and in summer—the sprinklers. And upon this vast and wondrous green walk barefoot lads, suntanned, tall and handsome like gods, and they sing, they march barefoot and they sing, they run along the paths, and vanish into the darkness of the orange groves . . . everywhere, all the time. . . . And this is a terrible danger, because there is jealousy around, and jealousy breeds hatred and in the sky black clouds appear. Notice, I said black. This is a completely different melody, which appears at the end of the *allegro* and it is a menacing melody, a kind of oriental melody. . . . Did you get the hint? An oriental melody, Arabic! This hint has to be understood. All the handsome lads have to go underground immediately. It is forbidden to go on running on the green earth. It is forbidden to sing aloud. It is forbidden to establish new settlements every day. Everything has to be done underground. For otherwise a great and dreadful betrayal will occur; the girls will be taken from the arms of the lovers; and in the other realm, my own, the same thing. . . . The *allegro* must end. Now comes an *andante* or an *adagio*, and everything is in the underground, in quiet, almost without a sound. But in the background the clouds will continue gathering in the sky, black clouds, note, black! And afterward there will come a terrible, cruel *scherzo*, with the sounds of wicked laughter . . . and blood will be shed . . . much blood. . . . It will be terrible, but it will end quickly and vanish. And then, once again a wonderful *allegro finale* . . . but that will come after much blood. . . . Listen well to what I am saying to you. Tell them to go underground and get ready. For now will come the age of blood, betrayal, and losses. . . . Everyone will lose what is dear to him, and afterward will have to build everything from within, anew. Have you understood me, Elyakum? I am speaking to you as man to man, whilst the woman sleeps and does not know a thing, because she is the earthly element, *pandemonia*, and we, you and I, are *panurania*. . . . I could have tried to demonstrate all this to you on the violin, but she would wake up, and then we would be back to the low earth, and the vision would vanish. . . . So I propose to you that we go outside, to the fields, with the violin. Come, Elyakum, come and hear something that no man has heard yet."

They walked down the slope of the hill, along the path where Elyakum and Liesl had walked on the night of their first meeting, and Amadeus Bieberkraut spoke as he walked. "I know people will not listen to me. They will not go underground, because they will say: Bieberkraut's gone mad. . . . They'll go on singing and walking upon the green earth, and then suddenly, at the end of the spring. . . . You can warn them, they will listen to you, because you live in a kibbutz and I live in a cave, you understand? . . . Here, we shall be able to play here."

They had reached a stone by the side of the orchard and Amadeus ordered Elyakum to sit down on the stone, and he himself took the violin out of the case and started to pluck on it.

Elyakum listened to the deluge of sounds borrowed from works he knew and from others he did not recognize, following upon each other in rapid tumult.

He played for a long time, and when he had finished

he put the violin back in its case. "Warn them," he said. "What I had to do I have done."

Beyond the orchard spots of dawn began to spread. As they returned together toward the hill, the houses of the kibbutz loomed like monsters crawling on the background of the clearing sky.

"They will burn everything you have," said Amadeus Bieberkraut, breathing heavily. "It will all go up in smoke, Elyakum. The pursuer will be pursued and the lover will be betrayed. The beautiful lads will shout and the beasts will migrate and wander. Flying birds sink in crevices of the great sea and the friends all drink blood. And I won't be here."

"All this time you've been with that madman?" asked Liesl, when Elyakum lay down on the bed beside her. "What did you talk about so long?"

"He plays well," said Elyakum. "He gave me an interesting explanation of music."

"They say that God saves the fools," said Liesl, before turning over on her side and falling asleep. "But I can't see it in your case."

"I'm not so sure," said Elyakum, but already Liesl did not hear.

In the middle of April 1936 the Arabs attacked the quarters close to Jaffa, and after that riots broke out all over the country and continued, with interruptions, until 1939, when the world war broke out.

One day, about a month after the outbreak of the 1936

riots, Elyakum read in a newspaper that the musician Amadeus Bieberkraut has been slaughtered in the cave where he dwelt. When his corpse was found it was seen that his sexual member had been tucked into his mouth.

At the end of the summer Liesl went to live in Meshulam Ha-Gelili's room. Elyakum, who had been recruited as a supernumerary policeman in the Galilee, learned about this from a brief letter, in which Liesl wrote, with dreadful spelling mistakes, about her decision and about the fact that she would always remember him and she asked him to forgive her. "In fect I shell be yoors, but only in a spiritual mannar, like a sister or a cousin"— wrote Liesl; and Elyakum read and re-read the letter, and finally he took a pencil and corrected *shell* to *shall* and *in fect* to *in fact* and *mannar* to *manner*, then tore the letter up into tiny fragments and dispersed them through the window.

When his service came to an end Elyakum traveled to his grandfather and stayed in the settlement for about a month. At first he wanted to join those who fought in the Civil War in Spain, but it was complicated and difficult. Finally Ephraim, with a heavy heart, agreed to find his grandson a position as a clerk in the London office of the Citrus-Growers' Association.

In the autumn Elyakum sailed to England and the Association notified Ephraim of his grandson's arrival in the office; but a week later Ephraim received another letter and in it it was said that Elyakum Ben-Zion had

notified them that he was retiring from the work and did
not leave an address.

22.

IN THOSE DAYS Herzl—the sole offspring of Ephraim and
Rivka—was thirty-nine years old and he had not taken a
wife. He lived in a bungalow for him alone, in Ephraim's
yard, dealing in the business of citrus orchards and other
orchards. Herzl was a tall man, bony and muscular, ele-
gantly attired in the style of England, as he had learned
and seen from the British officers of the Palestine Police.
He traveled regularly to Europe, and had established
friendly connections with fruit agents and British police
officers, who came from Palestine on home leave. He
wholeheartedly carried out missions for the Haganah
and occasionally he managed to arrange the release of
Jewish prisoners. Nevertheless, he was suspected by
those of the Haganah, both because he was a farmer's
son and because he dressed like one of the English and
was in their company at night, drinking with them in
hotel bars.

Herzl knew that he was not trusted by the institutions
of the Jewish population, and this amused him, because
in his heart he was far from them and, just like his father,
expected the day when the leaders of the workers would
step down from their positions of power, and the citizens
would take the reins of the regime into their own hands.

And in the meantime he did not mind serving the Jewish population indirectly, until their eyes would open to see that salvation would not come from the workers.

He was a silent man by nature, a man who walked solitary, took an odd comfort from the things that he saw and knew, without telling them to anyone. And when Ephraim gave him the task of finding Elyakum who had vanished in London, he fulfilled his duty, but did not reveal to anyone what he had discovered in his searches. He found Elyakum in London, about two years after his traces had been lost, among a group of English communists, living in a small commune on the south bank of the river, absorbed in studies of Marxism and making a living by working in the printing shop of the communist newspaper.

When Herzl found that Elyakum spoke English well, his mind was at rest.

"Please make the acquaintance of my uncle," said Elyakum to his friends. "He is a farmer from Palestine, an owner of orchards, and belongs to the class in which all my family is counted."

Herzl nodded to those present and did not even smile, but when he parted from Elyakum he gave him fifty pounds, which were immediately slipped into the funds of the commune.

At the Seder dinner of Passover 1939, the family gathered, as it did each year, in Ephraim's house. Rivka had her hands full with work, and even though she was almost sixty-nine, she did all the kitchen work with her own hands, helped by two Arab girls who were not

permitted to touch the pots and dishes, only to peel po-
tatoes and clean the vegetables.

Sarah and Aminadav arrived from Tel Aviv early in
the day, and their son Oved with his wife Rachel and
their two children—the four-year-old Uri and the three-
year-old Bella-Yaffa—came from Jerusalem near the
hour of sunset. And only when they were all gathered in
Ephraim's sitting room did Herzl emerge from his bungalow in the yard, dressed in gray flannel trousers and a
jacket the color of rust. He gave his brother Aminadav
and his nephew Oved a slap on the shoulders, and only
when he bent down to kiss Rachel and the children did
he take the pipe out of his mouth. At last he approached
his sister Sarah and embraced her by the shoulders, shar-
ing in her sorrow, leaning over her from the height of his
stature and asking her in a whisper if she had had any
news from her younger son, Elyakum. Sarah shook her
head and told him what she always said to anyone who
asked her about Elyakum: "I know in my heart that I am
guilty for all the trouble. If I had only been patient with
him, he would not have left home."

"We'll find him," Herzl promised her and put the pipe
back in his mouth, and immediately took his nephew
Oved by the arm, led him to a sofa at the back of the
room and the two of them launched into a conversation
on matters of law related to *Miri* lands and *Mulk* lands.*

---

*According to Ottoman law, *Miri* lands were leased lands owned
by the government, and *Mulk* lands were freehold lands belonging
completely to the buyer.

Oved was the only one in the entire family to whom Herzl behaved with any closeness, and at times they would even converse in English. Had Oved asked Herzl about his brother Elyakum, Herzl would surely have told him about their meeting in London. But as Oved did not ask, Herzl saw himself exempt from passing information. Herzl treated Ephraim with a certain degree of mercy: after every visit he made to London he would intimate to him that he was sure that Elyakum was alive and well, because people knew him, although they did not know his address, and one day he would be found hale and hearty. And Ephraim would tell Rivka and she would be calmed. But for his stepbrother Aminadav Herzl felt a loathing in his heart, and almost did not talk to him at all. And if he did happen to look at Aminadav, he would immediately see in his mind's eye the scene of lovemaking, twenty-seven years earlier, when he had come upon his sister Sarah in the stable. And then he would hold his breath for a moment and the pipe in his mouth would go out, and he would draw a box of matches from his jacket pocket and with a sour expression would busy himself for a long while with refilling the pipe and lighting it.

When they sat down to the Passover table there was an empty chair to Ephraim's right. A chair was ready and waiting for Elyakum, in case he changed his mind and returned suddenly to the family table. Grandmother Rivka squinted from time to time at the empty chair and shed a tear, whilst Sarah, Elyakum's mother, said that this was not a Jewish custom; and as for the symbolism, the symbol was defective, because Elyakum was surely seated at a Passover table in London, and what did he need two chairs for?

Ephraim conducted the Passover Seder according to all the prescriptions and fine points of the book of the Haggadah, and that year little Uri asked the Four Questions for the first time in his life. His grandmother, Sarah, promised his mother, Rachel, that to mark this occasion the grandson would receive a gift, a golden sovereign. And Rivka, his great-grandmother, again shed a tear, of joy.

Rachel *née* Cordoviero announced to all around the table that next year they would have to forego the presence of Oved and his family, since it was their duty to give some pleasure also to Grandfather and Grandmother Cordoviero in Jerusalem, as Uri was their firstborn grandson and they longed to hear him ask the Four Questions. To this Ephraim said, "We shall see."

After the dinner Herzl retired to his bungalow, and Ephraim's large house swallowed up the members of the family in the empty rooms, and stillness and darkness came down upon the yard. And in his bedroom Ephraim lay with closed eyes and three figures were competing amongst themselves to come before him and to say what they had to say; and he was embarrassed and apologetic, because he did not want to turn away Na'aman, who was buried in Paris, before Bella-Yaffa's disembodied soul; nor did he know if he were entitled to ask Elyakum to wait his turn, because he was alive, as far as was known, somewhere in England.

"Wait for me, my dears," he was slowly murmuring to himself, "soon, in a little while, I am with you."

Less than five months after the Passover the Second World War broke out, and between the spring and the autumn of that year Oved managed to finish a large business deal in real estate, and bought himself thirty acres of orchards and rocky land outside the settlement of Zichron Ya'acov, on the lower reaches of a hill overlooking Wadi Millk.

There were some vines, lots of fig and pomegranate trees, clumps of sabra cactus, acacia trees, and an ancient Arab ruin, bordering on a donkey track at the foot of the hill.

In spring, when Oved had begun his negotiations to buy the land, it was flowering wildly with cyclamens, crocuses, anemones, and abundant wild grasses; and in autumn, when the contract was signed and the war broke out, most of the area was stricken with yellow and gray blight. But Oved was not sorry about this. One way or the other the land was meant for parceling, to be sold to contractors who would build a cluster of villas on it. Agriculture is something for Grandfather Ephraim, Oved said to his wife Rachel.

But just as the Second World War broke out Grandfather Ephraim withdrew from agriculture and sealed himself within his house, listening to the radio and reading newspapers.

"What did I tell you then, in Alexandria?" he would exclaim triumphantly to his wife Rivka.

But Rivka did not remember, and it was necessary to bring Herzl into the room to bear witness.

"Well, Herzl, what did I say in Alexandria, while they were having their first war?" Ephraim urged his son.

And when it became apparent that Herzl too had been afflicted with forgetfulness, Ephraim reminded them of the lesson he had propounded then:

"Already then I told you that the Jewish population was divided into workers and farmers. Now they're calling it Socialists and Fascists. You and I—the Fascists; whilst those who eat from the table of the national funds are the Socialists. And what are the one and the other doing? A ship of Jews, refugees from Europe, arrives, and the people want to enter our land and find a refuge. The British army comes and fires on the ship. Hitler shoots at them in Europe and the British shoot at them in Asia. Our people, whom they're calling Fascists, went and blew up a British police station in Haifa. It was not pleasing to our people the Socialists, so they promptly caught some Fascists and informed on them to the English and imprisoned them in a concentration camp in Africa. Which is precisely what the workers did to the NILI people in the first war. So, who was right? Not I?"

The lawyer Oved Ben-Zion enlisted as a volunteer in the British army to fight Hitler, but his uncle Herzl, who continued to dress like an Englishman, became a secret accomplice of the Irgun Tzevai Leumi.* He bribed British policemen and bought weapons from them for the Irgun and also used to hide wounded men from the Irgun on his father's farm in the settlement; he also brought a physician for them, and he also dug a hiding place for weapons under the storehouses and the packing shed in the orchard. In the well a special ladder was installed and an oblique tunnel was dug; here too weapons were hidden, and sometimes men as well.

When Oved arrived on leave from the army, he hired several Arabs from the village Faradis, which was near the land he had bought, and ordered them to grow vegetables in the rocky land and among the trees. And since vegetables were in great demand, and as if it were part of the war effort, he received a financial subsidy from the national funds and thus by the end of the war had accumulated a tidy sum from this land, from the piece of land that was to be sold for building villas when the peace came. His father, Aminadav, opened a sewing workshop for military uniforms and sold the British huge quantities of khaki trousers and khaki shirts and khaki socks from the products of his own textile factory and the sewing workshop. His brother Herzl also traded with the army, since the orange markets in the world had closed, and he sold fruit to jam factories. Only Ephraim remained sealed within his house, reading

---

*National Military Organization, also known by its acronym "Etzel," the extremist right-wing underground military organization of the Jewish population in Palestine.

newspapers and listening to the radio. Once a week he would go to a meeting of the Citrus-Growers' Association, and if he was fortunate he managed to thread it with a speech about current events, to prove to the people that already in Alexandria he had seen what would happen.

Rachel's family, the Cordoviero tribe, continued cultivating their connections with their Arab friends and partners in Jerusalem. Complete understanding reigned in a small and exclusive circle of land brokers: all of them agreed among themselves that the British were to blame for all the troubles. Before they started inciting hatred and bitterness the Arabs and Jews had dwelt in peace side by side. Soon the British would be expelled, and peace between cousins would endure for ever, as in times past.

But in the innermost chambers of their own homes the Cordovieros were close in spirit to the zealots and contributed sums of money to the funds of the LEHI,* and also to the Irgun, whilst some of Rachel's brothers and uncles were members of the moderate Haganah, and some of them served in the British army, to fight against Hitler, the common enemy.

At the very same time the Arab friends of the

---

*The Fighters for the Freedom of Israel, whom the British nicknamed the "Stern Gang"—the most fanatic Jewish underground movement in Palestine, which did not refrain from engaging in personal terror.

Cordovieros were supporting the establishment of the Najadah, the underground military organization of the Arabs, so that when the time came there would be those who would fight the Jews and throw them into the sea, as was the command of the Mufti, Haj Amin-Al-Husseini, who in the meantime had fled the country and settled in Germany. The Arabs had newspapers with photographs showing Haj Amin inspecting a German regiment in the company of Hitler in person. One copy of such a newspaper arrived once by post to the Cordoviero family, without an additional word, and they guessed, more or less, who among their Arab friends had bothered to send them such a hint.

Apart from two chance bombings of Tel Aviv, by Italian planes, there were no casualties of the Second World War in Palestine. Like the Abramson family during the days of their stay in Alexandria in the First World War, the Jewish population was ready and willing to wait patiently until the Gentiles would finish killing each other for the reasons known to them alone. And indeed it is possible that the war would have been pictured in this way by the sons of the Jewish settlement, had not Hitler sought to destroy the Jews of Europe. News about the concentration camps and the gas chambers began infiltrating drop by drop, and not all at once was the truth passed on.

But when what was known became known—although only in part—it was no longer possible to sit back with arms folded and wait for the end of the war. And once again Ephraim Abramson summoned Rivka and Herzl to his room and declared to them:

"Well, ladies and gentlemen, who was right? They slaughter Jews in Europe, and the English shoot at refugee ships, but the workers tell us: Don't kill the English; the workers say to us: Our weapons are untainted. Who ever heard of weapons which are untainted? Weapons are created to ruin and destroy! Herzl, arise and do what you ought to do. In Alexandria you asked me if you should join the spies. Now I say to you: join the Irgun Tzvai Leumi, do you hear?"

"Father," said Herzl, "the workers' Haganah knows what it is doing. It isn't trying to destroy the Irgun. It's only bleeding a bit of its blood, but it lets it operate. In this way, all working together, we will get the cart out of the mud. That's the dirty game of politics."

"Don't betray the farmers," Ephraim warned him. "You're talking like one of the workers."

"Between the workers and the farmers there's room enough for me," Herzl replied to his father.

And whilst the Jews fought their wars within and without, the world war came to an end. Fifty million people perished in it, among them six million Jews. But the British did not permit the survivors to enter the Land of Israel.

"Now there is no alternative," said Ephraim to his wife Rivka and to his son Herzl. "Now we must declare open and clear-cut revolt."

"The revolt has already been declared," said Herzl. "How is it that you have not noticed, Father?"

"Has it been reported in the papers?" asked Ephraim in amazement.

"If they did not write it yet, they will write it now," promised Herzl.

And verily during those days an illegal placard was issued by the Haganah, stating explicitly, "Let our moans be hearkened unto from the abysses of quiescence!"

The English at police headquarters, and those in the High Commissioner's palace, were sure that they were hearing hollow phraseology. They did not understand that there is a nation among the nations ready to die for its phraseology, both because it had been offended and because it lacked experience in international politics.

The English also did not know this: that the Jews are a pragmatic people, and they have an important precept they apply—a man will always try to fit his principles to reality, but if that is difficult, then he will fit the reality to his principles.

And since the British authorities did not know any of this, their end was that they were kicked and flung out of the Land of Israel; and the story is known.

In the spring of 1946 the telephone rang in Herzl's hut. Elyakum spoke at the other end: "Hello, Uncle Herzl. I've come back to the Land of Israel."

"And your communists, what did they have to say about that?" Herzl wanted to know.

"Is it possible to come to you at home?" said Elyakum.

"Of course," Herzl said. And immediately he went to tell Ephraim.

"I told you," Ephraim mumbled. "Indeed I have said it all the time."

In the evening Sarah and Aminadav arrived too. Oved, Elyakum's brother, rang from Jerusalem and apologized that he could not come because he was busy.

Elyakum answered his questioners with a condensed and short sentence: "It was hard," he said. They could get nothing more out of him. On the other hand he asked them to lend him a little money, so he could tour the country and see the changes.

"You always gave him money," Sarah said to her father, "and you saw what has come of it. So give him some now too."

"And how!" Ephraim taunted her. "As much as he asks for. The boy's cured of all his madness."

"How do you know?" Sarah wanted to know, surveying her son with evident fear.

"This can be seen immediately," said Ephraim. "If he had come back to the bosom of the motherland, it means that he is cured. . . . You don't intend to go back to the kibbutz?" He turned to Elyakum in sudden alarm.

"Only for a courtesy visit," Elyakum said. "Just to say hello."

And within a day Elyakum took off from the house just as he had come. It was Herzl who drove him in his car to the gate of the kibbutz. "You did well not to tell them about our meeting in London," Herzl said.

"You learned one thing over there after all—to keep
learned one thing over there after all—to keep silent."

"You didn't tell them that we met?" said Elyakum in
astonishment.

"You didn't ask me to tell them," replied Herzl, and
waved good-bye.

In the kibbutz he was told that Meshulam Ha-Gelili
had departed from this world and that Liesl had left the
place even before his death. Of the entire group which
had arrived from Germany only a handful of boys and
girls remained, and from them Elyakum obtained Liesl's
address. She was married, to a carpet merchant from
among the Jews of Bukhara, an extremely rich man of
about sixty.

"Liesl," Elyakum said into the receiver, inside a telephone booth in Tel Aviv, "do you recognize my voice?"

"Child, is it you? What a surprise! Why don't you
come over right away? Just don't get a fright. I'm terribly
fat, and also old. Have a glass of cognac before you
come."

Liesl's husband, Mr. Babayoff, heard that Elyakum
had been in London and became excited. He wanted to
know if Elyakum knew Knightsbridge. He had a brother
there, Mr. Babayoff, also a carpet dealer, and his shop
had been bombed during the war but had already been
restored. Elyakum spoke at length with Mr. Babayoff
and answered all his questions, and from time to time he
glanced at Liesl and saw her sitting in the armchair, her

hands in her lap, her face full and calm. Only her eyes seemed to be pleading for something.

When the telephone rang and Mr. Babayoff left the room, Elyakum said, "Why did you go to Meshulam Ha-Gelili?"

Liesl reached out both hands to him and said, "Eli, give me a kiss."

"Why did you go to Meshulam?" he repeated, and did not move from his place.

"You still don't understand? Till now you don't understand?"

"If I understood, I would not have asked," said Elyakum.

"If you don't understand, it would be futile for me to try to explain," said Liesl. "Why don't you want to give me a kiss?"

Mr. Babayoff returned to the room, and offered apologies for his absence.

Elyakum stood up from his chair, bowed toward Liesl, shook hands with Babayoff, and went out into the street.

In the street a large demonstration was streaming by and at the head of the large demonstration there was displayed a large placard and on it was written, "Let our moans be hearkened unto from the abysses of quiescence!"

For a while Elyakum stood watching the marching people and the British police who were escorting the crowd and afterward he went to the bus station and returned to his grandfather's house. Elyakum was thirty-two years old when he returned home, and he did not know why he had returned.

"Don't be in a hurry," Grandfather Ephraim said to him. "Take your time. We will make a plan."

"I have no plans," Elyakum replied to him.

"I will make them for you, don't worry," promised Ephraim. "I won't let you rot in your father's factories. . . . All of a sudden he's gone and become a tailor, uniforms for the army he began to sew. That's not for you. I will arrange something good for you, here in the settlement."

"I have a teacher's certificate," Elyakum blurted out.

"What kind of teaching?" Ephraim was frightened.

"I'm a teacher of Marxism," Elyakum explained. "I studied and I was given a certificate."

"Marxism? That's like the Bolsheviks. . . . You forget about that. In our family there's no such thing. . . . You listen to me carefully and then you will decide for yourself. . . . For example, your uncle Herzl should have taken on an assistant long ago, and if you don't want that, you could start something in the Association, but this time it will be here, at home; there's no need to run far. . . . You sit calm, there's time, no one is putting any pressure on you. . . . You are no longer a child, Eli. You are by now how old? And also marriage should have been thought of a long time ago, and you shouldn't worry about that either."

"I'm not worried," said Elyakum. "I just don't know what, exactly."

Requiem for Na'aman

And when people do not know, history comes and takes care of them and sets up opportunities for them and sometimes history fulfills its mission by proxy. Elyakum, for example, met history in the form of a bespectacled communist leader with a mustache, who explained to him that on the soil of Palestine there would soon occur the first stage in the liquidation of the British Empire, and that one of the ways to take part in this historic process was to join the ranks of the LEHI; though a complex body in which there were Fascist elements, it could be bent and harnessed to the chariot of the revolution, and in its ranks there were already members who knew their tasks.

In 1947 Elyakum was already running and galloping in front of the chariot of the revolution and from what his comrades told him he learned that he was a brave hero, a valiant fighter, and a daring commander. All this, because he did not mind laying mines inside the barbed-wire fences of army camps, shooting from ambush, lying all night in a trench by the side of the road, or lying on a water tower and sniping from there at passing convoys of the English.

When he was off duty, he told his comrades about dialectical materialism and they did not laugh at him, because he was a hero; but they would slip out of the room one after the other. And when he remained alone, he would put records on the gramophone and listen to music. And if he found himself in the room of strangers, between one action and another, he would whistle all kinds of passages of music to himself, and so he acquired the nickname "Whistler," because when he was not speaking or being spoken to he would whistle melodies to himself.

With time, he stopped speaking; and in 1948, when the War of Independence broke out and the leaders declared the founding of the State of Israel, Elyakum was posted to Battalion 89. In December, during a charge on the entrances of the Negev, an Egyptian bullet hit him and killed him. From the Military Rabbinate three men were sent to notify his father and mother.

At the end of 1948 the number of war victims reached five thousand. And the dead left behind them bereaved parents and war widows. And in these large numbers there was the power of belonging; and from the power of belonging the road is not far to succumbing to fate. And from having succumbed it is only one step to the frozen face. Not to cry. Not to break. Those who fell did not fall in vain. Not like those millions of Jews who died in the crematoria. Here we know what we are being killed for.

The Abramsons and the Ben-Zions would read about all these things in the newspapers every day, and every day they would throw the newspapers aside fearfully and say, "Not upon us." And the Cordovieros would say, "Except us." And now this thing came and crept up and reached the threshold of the house and struck the people in the heart. Oved, the elder brother of the one slain, was summoned home from the army, where he was serving as a transport and supply officer. When they told him about his brother's death Oved felt outraged and humiliated. That such a thing should happen to him, to his family, was something that bordered on disgrace, a kind of insolence which, if allowed to pass in silence, was like admission to degradation of honor. And Oved did indeed speak words like spurs: "I will avenge this blood. I vow to avenge this blood," he repeated and said.

Ephraim sat shrunken up in his armchair and asked for his coat. He emphatically rejected the suggestion that he not go to the funeral. With his hands in the air he waved away the suggestion, but did not utter a sound. Rivka pinched her cheeks, until it became necessary to hold her for a long while; and Elyakum's mother, Sarah, sobbed in the arms of her husband Aminadav and kept repeating and saying to him that she did not want to live any more, that she was guilty for everything, that the child had, in fact, been an orphan from the day he was born, they had simply forgotten him, and now she did not want to live anymore. And Aminadav would pat her on the shoulder, shake her, and reply to her in a bewildered mumble and say, "Well, yes, I too. . . . What do you want, Sarah? I too. . . . What is it, what's the matter with you?"

Aminadav never spoke in long or ordered sentences. Nor did he know how to cry, as he did not know how to laugh. He was a man dedicated to his family and to his business, but he was not prepared at all for such a thing.

113

This was something new, and also not right. It had come as a surprise, with no preparation. How can you do a thing without being prepared? And did the others understand more than he? Or were they only pretending that they understood? If they were not so, why was it not revealed to him? Why was he so completely outside? Could it be that the others knew more about what had happened to Elyakum? Was not Elyakum his son? His son and not theirs. Well then, what?

When those accompanying the shrouded corpse reached the pit into which it was to be lowered, brief lightning was seen at the margins of the sky, and the sound of thunder was heard rolling in from afar, and the army rabbi looked at the sky, twisted up his face, and got down to the task without delay. Grandmother Rivka fell upon the wet clumps of earth beside the grave and began to weep bitterly and her daughter Sarah stooped over to lift her up, and when she did not succeed in this, she joined her and she too lay on the ground. Ephraim did not move from his place, looking at the corpse draped in white and saying things to himself in a whisper. He appeared not to have even noticed what his wife and daughter were doing. Rachel and Oved too stood to the side. And also Aminadav, Elyakum's father, did not interfere, because he thought that they were doing what had to be done, and perhaps he too ought to do something, but he did not know what. And then, as his eyes were wandering about, he saw his stepbrother, Herzl.

To the side Herzl was standing, separated from the

others, also different from them all in his attire and the height of his stature and the English mustache curling upward at the ends. And lo and behold, what do Aminadav's eyes see? Herzl sobbing out loud, without shame, his shoulders trembling, his mouth uttering stifled groans, and his bony frame swaying like a tree in the wind, a tree creaking and about to break. What was Elyakum to Herzl? In his heart Aminadav was alarmed. Had they struck up a kind of secret covenant between them? Or did Herzl understand that Aminadav does not know a thing, and therefore Herzl is doing what Aminadav ought to do? Or was this whole thing beyond Aminadav's understanding, because he does not exist at all? For if he did exist he would have known what to do. Aminadav tries to remember something important from his life, but apart from certain difficulties he is unable to recall anything, and he becomes still more alarmed. Is it possible that Herzl lives and exists in a different form to that in which Aminadav lives and exists? About the women one is not to pose questions, but Herzl is a man of action, a serious man; and lo and behold, look what he is doing here.

And into Aminadav's heart crept a terrible suspicion that perhaps it had all been a kind of mistaken bargain, and all that was, had been in the wrong direction, or without any direction at all. If Herzl frisks about like this, it means that he knows what he is breaking up about and what for, whilst Aminadav does not know a thing and nobody tells him. Or perhaps they had told him and he had not understood. All this time he had not understood. What did he have there, inside, in his breast? Aminadav listened within himself and suddenly it seemed to him that there was void. Perhaps it had been full once, perhaps it had been full only two or three days ago; but now, it seemed void. Absolutely nothing. His breathing became heavier and he swallowed air with his mouth gaping, so as to fill the empty space inside him, since a space cannot exist without being filled with something. And then his heart came to his assistance, and its muscles contracted toward the inner space within himself, contracted violently and there was no more need to swallow air. He collapsed where he stood, and the void was once again full.

People rushed to him, shook him, and some fool shouted for water to sprinkle on him, despite the rain that was pouring down now on Aminadav too, and on the clumps of earth that had been thrown over the corpse covered in shrouds.

Aminadav's death was reported to Rivka and Ephraim only several days later and Rivka lay in bed and refused to get up. Sarah, who had lost her son and become a widow in one day, left her empty house in Tel Aviv and came to the settlement to watch over her mother who was in bed and her father who sat in his armchair and did not speak; and Herzl went to Tel Aviv and spent several weeks in the offices of Aminadav's factories, and made some arrangements toward their sale.

Oved rang almost every day, from his army camp,

and his wife Rachel wrote a letter of condolence to each of the families and asked to be forgiven for not being able to come and be with them, because she had to look after the little ones Uri and Bella-Yaffa, especially since Uri was about to turn thirteen and she had to prepare his bar-mitzvah celebration, while his father was away somewhere, as is known. Only may he be healthy and return home, and may the terrible war finish and end at last. "Our family has given enough sacrifices"—Rachel finished both her letters with the same sentence; it is probable that owing to the vexations she was unable to express two separate ideas.

When Oved came home from his military service, he found an envelope addressed to him. Two soldiers from Elyakum's unit had brought it to his house the day after the funeral. In the envelope Oved found a copybook and according to what he peeked in and saw he understood that it was Elyakum's diary. He read here and there, and did not understand what the writing was about, but he also came across passages containing general views on public matters, and he did not find any interest in these. The notebook was laid in a drawer for several years. When Oved built himself a summerhouse near Zichron Ya'acov—as will be told further—he passed the notebook on to his daughter, Bella-Yaffa, because she was preoccupied with literature.

In the spring of 1949 the war ended. Ephraim sat facing the radio, listening to a speech by one of the ministers, who was summing up the battles and eulogizing the dead. The minister sounded the praises of men and women, and especially the youth. He mentioned kibbutzim in which nearly one-third of the kibbutz population had been killed or wounded. He mentioned families which had lost two, even three, sons. He singled out for praise the heroism of fathers who had joined the army to fill the places of their sons who had fallen; and Ephraim still expected and hoped for some mention, somehow, even only a hint, of his grandson Elyakum and perhaps even his son, Aminadav; but the minister moved quickly on to other matters. Ephraim turned off the radio and turned around, to say to Rivka what was in his heart, but remembered that there was no one to speak to. She was lying in bed and there was now no one to speak to. Then he said to himself, "How those workers hate us, the citizens and the farmers. Even when we are dead, we are not good enough for the radio. Kibbutzim, this yes, but Elyakum and Aminadav, they are not to be mentioned. Damn them. . . ."

"Did you want something, Father?" asked Sarah from the kitchen.

"Don't want a thing," said Ephraim.

Even so, he was not right. Two years later, when Rivka was no longer alive, and he was eighty-seven years old, the government decided to celebrate his birthday sumptuously. In those days, in 1952, the arrival of the first pioneers in the Land of Israel was seventy years old; and since hardly any of them remained alive, Ephraim Abramson was thought of as a kind of representative of that generation. And as for why Ephraim was chosen as the representative of this generation, and where the celebration was held, and who attended it—of all these things it will yet be told.

23.

IN THAT YEAR the plans for parceling the land Oved had purchased on the skirts of the hill were approved. A year later almost all the sections of land had been sold and then Rachel said a very reasonable thing to her husband: "Why should we sell it all and not leave ourselves a single section? Isn't it a very beautiful place?"

So Rachel and Oved drove out to their land, parked beside the ruins of an Arab house, and went for a walk in the area. They were experienced people, Rachel and Oved, and it was not hard for them to see that the half-acre rising on a gentle and pleasant slope from the main road was the most beautiful section of all, and that the Arab ruin lent it an additional touch of charm and ancient splendor. When they would build their summerhouse there, they would not destroy the ruin, but they would restore it and it would be a kind of pavilion inside the garden and there it would be possible to drink coffee or roast mutton over coal. All they had to do was to reinforce the shaky stones with plaster and assemble a pergola of wooden beams in place of a roof; and on the walls would climb a grape vine. It would be desirable for this vine to be the Dabuki sort, which is a species of many branches, strong and abounding in large clusters. This matter would be determined by Grandfather Ephraim, who was an expert on vines. And in fact, why shouldn't Grandfather Ephraim live in this house with his daughter Sarah all year round? It's not good for a house to remain empty of residents.

Thus, before the house had been raised, the plan was already complete and perfected. Rachel and Oved had thought everything out in advance, in every matter.

At the beginning of 1951 the furniture was taken out of the old house in the settlement. Among the furniture was the piano which the Baron Rothschild had given to Rivka's first husband, that piano on which Na'aman had started playing when he was still a little boy.

Only Herzl remained alone on the estate, in his bungalow in the yard. Ephraim and his daughter Sarah, she who was the mother of Oved, moved to the new summerhouse near Zichron Ya'acov and there they dwelt until the day of their death.

It was a spacious house, that had a cloister of arches surrounding it on all sides, and it was coated with rough plaster, in Italian village style, but inside it was fitted with all the innovations of technology and electricity. The ruin too was restored with fine craftsmanship. When the laborers came to clean away the rubble of stone, a human skeleton was discovered beneath the heap. Oved was called to the place, and immediately considered: if he were to inform the police that a skeleton had been found, there would be inquiries and perhaps even delays in the building. On the other hand, it was possible that this was a Jewish skeleton, and it is forbidden to throw it out into the wadi. Therefore he ordered a Roman sarcophagus that was found up the hill to be dragged down, and the sarcophagus was brought into the garden and placed beside the ruin; and the crumbling skeleton was thrown into the sarcophagus. Clumps of earth were thrown on it, until it was full of earth, as a kind of flower pot. And in that earth geranium bushes were planted, and they quickly burst forth in an abundance of red and pink blossoms; some time later two cypresses were planted on either side of the sarcophagus, for the sake of symmetry. The secret of the skeleton was known only to the workers and to Oved. The workers departed in the end, and Oved did not tell anyone, because there is no need to tell saddening stories.

Oved was a great believer in the rebirth of the nation, and saw himself as a sort of model and exemplar of the simple healthy principles of the ideal: a healthy mind in a healthy body, the Maccabean motto. As for the body —he took care to swim every day in the pool and to play tennis once a week. And as for the mind—he would push aside all books and plays which were not entertaining, to keep sorrow away from the heart.

The other principle in which Oved believed was the

readiness to make sacrifices for the sake of the ideal (during the war he had lost his brother and several of his closest friends, and one of his wife's cousins also fell in the war). He also believed in proper education for children, and for this reason in the evenings his house was always full of paragons, so that the children, Uri and Bella-Yaffa, might see and learn: generals in the army, war heroes, war cripples, and heroes of the underground that had been before the founding of the State. They would tell their stories, eat, and drink, and the children would listen and pay heed.

Since Oved was faithful to these principles, he himself became trusted and accepted by people and institutions at the center of life; this in spite of the fact that he was a son of sons of farmers and not of workers, not of the workers who had established the kibbutzim and the workers' party. Ephraim was too old to be aware of his grandson's betrayal of the citizens; and if he did notice for a moment, he immediately forgot. Most of the time his mind was given over to his memories, and the year 1951 would suddenly become for him 1918 and he would sometimes say peculiar things. But Oved loved his grandfather and instructed his children, Uri and Bella-Yaffa, to treat him with great respect. But the great-grandson and the great-granddaughter did not need their father's instructions. Their souls clave unto Ephraim's soul, and everything he told them was beautifully accommodated by them and they found no contradictions or surprises in his tales of Turkish gendarmes who were mounted on camels and fought against people of the Palmach, with Yosef Trumpeldor at their head.* Ephraim told the children about Absalom Feinberg,† who had set out alone into the desert where he had met the Ten Lost Tribes, and to this day he was the leader of their regiments, charging out at night at the head of his men whenever there was an hour of trouble to Israel, and striking at the English, the Arabs, and the Turks.

Most of all Uri and Bella-Yaffa loved the story about the boy Na'aman, whose hair floated on the surface of the river whilst he himself lived under water and there played on a piano. One day Bella-Yaffa showed Ephraim a drawing she had made and in it could be seen the boy Na'aman playing before the king of the water; and so Bella-Yaffa also read Ephraim a poem she had composed in honor of the boy Na'aman.

And these are the fits of the poem:

> In the realm of the mute fishes
> Abides the dead boy Na'aman
> Upon the thin harp strands he plays
> And to the artist all hearken.
>
> His hair hovers on the waters
> His spirit hovers in the world
> And in heaven listen the angels
> But he's most beautiful of all.

---

*Turkish gendarmes were active only until 1917. The Palmach, the striking force of the Haganah, was created only in 1940. Trumpeldor was killed by the Arabs in 1921.

†A Jewish spy who worked for the British as one of the NILI group of spies. He was lost in the desert in 1917, killed by Bedouins; his bones were found about fifty years later.

"Give me that," said Ephraim. "When I meet Na'aman, I will show him what you wrote."

"But only Na'aman," said Bella-Yaffa. "Because it's not for publication."

Bella-Yaffa wrote many poems, but she did not show them to anyone. Whenever she listened to the things told by the generals, heroes, and cripples in her father's house, her heart would fill with a terrible sorrow, and she would want to console these people and to caress them. But she did not move from her place and did not say a thing, because the motions of her heart were completely private. Apart from that, she thought that all the sufferings of the heroes and the generals had been in vain, and so the sorrow was sevenfold greater. And why in vain? Because they ate and drank and made merry, and sometimes even used obscene language. Which proved that they had not understood at all what had happened to them. And if they did not understand, what did they do it for? This is how these things were pictured in Bella-Yaffa's heart, but these were things that she kept only to herself. And so she did not understand everything; and before one understands something thoroughly, what is the sense of telling another?

When Oved heard that there were preparations for national celebrations in honor of the seventieth anniversary of the arrival of the first pioneers, he approached some people in the government, and suggested that a celebration be held in honor of his grandfather, who was one of the remnants of that generation. He also proposed that the celebration be held in his summerhouse, and there would be invitations to the Prime Minister and the Ministers and the leaders and the representatives of the youth. And from words to deeds, as was Oved's custom; it was decided and agreed. To the list of invited guests Oved added several of the generals, heroes, underground members, and cripples. According to the plan the Prime Minister would open with a speech, and afterward there would be a dinner, and after the dinner the people would sit in the restored ruin and listen to stories of heroism and war adventures.

And so it was. Ephraim was set at the head of the gathering, and Ephraim agreed to all that was done, but he explicitly stipulated one condition, that it would be told about on the radio and reported about in the newspapers. And Oved said to him, "Rely on me, Grandfather, let it be upon my head. I'll take care of it."

When they invited Herzl to the party, he replied on the telephone that if he was free he might come.

Uri was permitted to bring to the party two of his friends from the Gymnasium, and Bella-Yaffa asked for and was given permission to bring her only friend, her teacher of literature, the Doctor Yonas-Yehoshuah Bieberkraut, the younger brother of the deceased musician, Amadeus Bieberkraut, who had been cruelly murdered in a cave during the 1936 riots.

Sixteen years old was Bella-Yaffa that year, and Yonas-Yehoshuah Bieberkraut was thirty-five years old, but in spite of that they had struck up a secret covenant between them. A private covenant, of course.

After the Prime Minister had finished presenting his speech, he got into his car and drove off to another gathering, and the Ministers drove after him, and in the summerhouse of Rachel and Oved there remained the generals, the heroes, and the cripples alone, with a handful of select guests. They all adjourned from the sitting room to the restored ruin and sat down on wicker stools, their glasses in their hands.

About then Uncle Herzl arrived and sat down on a stool, his back against the wall, sucking his pipe.

Hero A sipped some cognac from his glass and recounted:

"When the war started we found out that the Arabs were loading rifles and mortars on a ship in an Italian port, so we checked it out and it turned out that it was an actual fact. Just that. So they said to me: You are going there and using your peepers to see what can be done. So we bought a couple of suits, shirts, and neckties, and got dressed to kill and took off for Italy. We come; see; right. There is a ship there. Fact. What do we do? First thing I put Moti on twenty-four-hour lookout. Avrema'le went off to prepare a leech mine. God help him. We always said: Avrema'le should've gone and been a professor. Hands of gold and a head of iron. Stubborn like a donkey. I says to him: How'll you prepare a mine? He says to me: Trust me. He went off, got some newspapers, got a bottle, brought a detonator, filled the bottle with acid, wrapped it in newspapers. He didn't put a cork in the bottle. The acid'll come out of the bottle and he figured it out: it'll take eight hours for the acid to get the papers wet. After eight hours the detonator is activated. You've got eight hours—says Avrema'le to me. Says I: That's enough. In the night I swim out to the ship, and as I am about twenty meters from it I duck-dive, but I hold the mine above the water. And when I touch the side of the ship, I attach the mine. Swim back diving twenty meters under water, and come out of the water. Dark. Several Italianos are standing around up top. We've finished. We go to the hotel, sit in the window and wait. An hour, two, five hours. The suspense, as they say, increases. Six hours, seven hours and now eight—where's the explosion, where is the watermelon? Nothing. Avrema'le—I says to him—some professor, where's the explosion? There's no Avrema'le. He's silent like the dead. Ashamed. We wait. Nervous. Almost nine hours. We have practically given up as all of a sudden we hear such a boom, that we jump to our feet. Looking. The ship, like nothing's happened. Avrema'le—I says to him—what'd you put in the mine? Aubergine salad? And just as I am laughing at him, the ship, so to say, starts to tilt a bit to the side, and hop, a bit more to the side. And we hear shouting from the harbor. Pals—I says—let's move. And that was it. The *Argirro* went shitting. He sank in the sea. That was the name of the ship. My foot got smashed in a different operation. But first let somebody else tell something."

Hero B sipped from his glass of cognac and recounted:

"People say there's no such thing as fate. I say there is. You want proof? Please. We went to capture the crossroads. Between Hatta and Haratiyah. We were supposed to meet at Huleikath. I check out my unit and see Chaim the Redhead. I say to him: You, go home. It's enough that your brother was lost to you a month ago. One doesn't try one's luck. So Chaimke he says to me: Is that an order or a suggestion? I say to him: Don't be cleverer than fate. Get going. He didn't go. You're not going? No need. I meant only good. Are we off? We're off. What went on there I don't need to tell you. It's known what went on there. At Huleikath I ask: Where's Chaimke? No Chaimke. What happened? Kicked the bucket? Nobody knows. I'm not sparing my efforts. I insist and ask everybody. They don't know. I say to myself: What am I going to tell his father? Where'll I get the courage? I decided to go out into the field. I went alone. If two go it makes easy work for those Sudanese snipers. So I went one. Walk, walk. What do you see in the dark? You see black. My foot hits something, I bend down, nothing. Another hit, I bend down, a dead Egyptian. By the uniform and the rifle, you can tell even at night. I go on. Firing? There's firing. I lie down. I crawl. I crawl and the whoresons keep firing. No shortage of ammunition there. As I crawl, a body. Warm, breathing, motherfucker. What if he grabs his gun and finishes me off? No choice. I say: Who's that? What do I hear? Chaimke. If he recognized me, I don't know. But he hadn't forgotten Hebrew. I say to him: How are things?

He said: Shit. I said: Good. Relax. From here to there they got fed up with firing. I start dragging him along the ground, crawling. Firing again. And also Chaimke's saying it hurts him. What do you expect. With a bullet in the belly, of course it hurts. Fine, I turned him over, carefully, onto his back. Feel better now? I crawl, dragging him. Not talking. What's there to talk about? I told him before we left, didn't I. He didn't agree. He wanted to be a Samson? Fine. Words are superfluous. We crawl. It went on like that for about an hour, maybe an hour-and-a-half. In the end we got there, he got an injection, they washed his wound. Today he works at Solel Boneh Contracting Company. Good luck to him. But I told him ahead of time, only he was lucky and I wasn't right one hundred percent, only fifty. Of course I didn't come out of it untouched. I copped two bullets while we were crawling. That's my medal. I don't think I derserve it. But they gave it to me, so what the hell. If they give you something, take it. There were guys who deserved a lot more and never got it. It's all a matter of fate. A bastard, that Chaimke. He's a foreman."

Hero C sipped from the cognac glass in his hand and recounted:

"Here we're talking about fine deeds. All honor to them. But get this: all these deeds were done by guys who'd been given an education and training and practice to do heroic deeds. So what's the wonder? If a strong healthy lout like Yoske goes out to save a wounded man, crawling there and back under fire, then fine, all honor to him. But he'll surely agree with me that it's the natural thing for him to do. What else is expected of him? That he should invent Einstein's theory? So what I want to say is something else. Let's look and see what people without such training did. Why look far? They say that Safed is a town of Kabbalah and mystery and all sorts of things like that. All right. Well I'll tell you that Safed and Jerusalem and Tiberias are places of loafers and all kinds of sissies. But there too, there's all kinds. And if I suddenly discover that in Safed there lives a Jew who deserves a medal, then he should be given a medal, even if he has a beard and sidelocks. I'm talking about Zilber, the one with the shop of kitchen wares. Yes. Zilber. Not Uri, not Yoske, not Chaim the Redhead, just someone called Zilber. Why look far? Take the days before the State, when we brought in illegal immigrants through Syria and Lebanon on donkeys. I'm not talking about the good guys who risked their lives and did their job. I'm not talking about what happened afterward, when the British police caught the immigrants and were going to send them off to God knows where. So here appears this old Jew, I wouldn't have given a penny for him, and he goes to the chief of police, a shitty and self-important British officer. And whatever kinds of whores the English were, one thing I have to say in their favor: they saw in Zilber something that we didn't grasp at all. If you met him in the street, you'd say: Just another one of those black cockroaches. But the Englishman understood something entirely different. He grasped that here he had to do with something very ancient and strong as a rock. Zilber was not someone to be shouted at. Not to be put in the clink or beaten either. You had to decide, either you don't take any notice of him, or you take your hat off to him. So the Englishman took off his hat. And what did this Zilber do, all in all? He goes to the police and says that he is putting down bail for the immigrants and demands their release. You think the English say no? They say yes. Why? Because if you offer an Englishman something legal, they accept it. Zilber is offering bail money—well that is fine. Sign, Zilber, sign for one thousand pounds and the immigrant goes free. The immigrant promises to appear for trial on a specific day; if he doesn't appear before the judge, Zilber loses a thousand pounds for every immigrant. Do you know what sums Zilber signs for? Millions! And do you know how many immigrants appear before the judge? Bugger all! Not one. Zero immigrants. What then? According to British law the officer has to go to Zilber and demand the money. But he doesn't go. And where does Zilber get the chutzpah to keep coming back every day and sign bail for more immigrants? That is the question. Where does he have the chutzpah from? And the answer is: From his faith. You and I don't see it, but that whoreson Englishman sees it, and every time that Zilber comes, the Englishman says: Please, bastard, sign. Here, down below, on this form. And Zilber signs and goes home to his shop, owing another million. You would ask: What's the heroism in it? If the Englishman doesn't demand the money from him, why shouldn't he go on signing until the end of the world? Well I'll tell you: what's heroic about it is that Zilber's a believing Jew, a religious man as they say, without tricks. For him God is God, sin is sin, and a lie is a lie. And the Torah forbids lying, and nevertheless, to save Jews, he lies about millions of pounds. He's really, according to his faith, ordering his place in hell, to be roasted on a small fire. That's the crux of the matter. This is his heroism. But if you ask me, and even though I'm not a rabbi and don't know a bloody thing about religious matters and all that, I'll tell you that not only isn't this Zilber going to any damned hell, but he'll be taken to Paradise in a Cadillac, and I don't know that even God himself might not come and open the door for him, if there's a door there, and if at all. All I know is that his family name isn't Zilber anymore, it's Kaspi.* He went and made a Hebrew name for himself. In honor of the State. So they won't just say Ben-Gurion and Sharet. So there'll be Kaspi too. All honor to him."

Yonas-Yehoshuah Bieberkraut, who sat nearby, turned pale and leapt to his feet.

"With your permission, ladies and gentlemen, I would like to have permission to speak."

All the faces turned toward him and saw immediately that he was not one of the heroes or the generals. His huge nose, the head large for his body, the pallor of his

---

*It means the same thing: "silver."

face and his diminutive stature, as well as his attire, which looked as if it had been brought in a parcel from the Twenties, attested that he did not belong here, or, in fact, any other specific place in this country.

"Mr. Ben-Zion, with your permission, may I say a few words?" said Bieberkraut to Oved.

"Please do," said Oved. "Gentlemen, Doctor Bieberkraut is the teacher of literature at our daughter's Gymnasium. Please go ahead, Doctor Bieberkraut, it is an honor for us."

"Well, I, that is," began Yonas-Yehoshuah, the brother of the murdered Amadeus, "I have been listening studiously, both out of respect and courtesy. . . . When the Prime Minister and the Ministers were here, already then I should have asked permission to speak, but they left all of a sudden, and now I have to do an indecent thing, to speak about people behind their backs. . . . But you surely meet them, and you will be able to pass it on to them. . . . I despise them in my heart just as Michal, daughter of Saul, despised David in her heart, when he was leaping and dancing before the Ark of the Lord and let his spittle fall down upon his beard. . . . I despise all the politicians, because they're despicable, and there is no need to elaborate on it. . . . Not you, gentlemen, not you. You I respect with all my heart, because you are down-to-earth, foundation stones, pillars of society, and bear the burden and carry the suffering. . . . You are the victims of a moment of cruel history, every one with one of his hands wrought in the work and the other held a weapon. . . . My martyred brother too, may God avenge his blood, in one of his hands he held the violin and he was killed at the hands of villains. . . . It is not this that I want to speak about. . . . I have only come to remind you as briefly as possible, to remind you of something which should never be allowed to pass into oblivion. . . . Our strength is in the spirit, not in muscles. Gentlemen, the Jewish people has only one front . . . over against Mount Sinai . . . art, gentlemen, and love thy neighbor as thyself, in hymns, all that man is, alone he is born and alone he dies, and so love, spirit. . . . I beg your forgiveness, gentlemen, thank you very much for your kind attention."

And just as he had leapt up from his place so he returned and sat down, and concealed his face between the palms of his hands.

Bella-Yaffa caressed his hand and whispered something in his ear. At the same time the guests smiled openly and someone said to Oved that it would be worthwhile for him to take his daughter out of this Gymnasium and send her to another Gymnasium. Many burst out laughing and Yonas-Yehoshuah and Bella-Yaffa got up from their places and fled from the restored ruin toward the house. Rachel hurried after them and Ephraim—who had been drowsing up until now—woke to the sounds that had arisen around him and smiled affably at the people who were beside him.

"Bravo, Mr. Abramson," several of the generals and

the heroes said to him, "how wonderful you look for your age. We could wish the same."

And verily the next day a notice appeared in the newspaper about the party at the summerhouse of lawyer Oved Ben-Zion, and on the radio it was told about briefly and Ephraim's name was mentioned explicitly.

"You see, Grandfather," said Rachel to Ephraim as they listened to the radio together in the sitting room, "Oved promised and kept his promise. You heard it spelled out: Ephraim Abramson."

"They're cunning," smiled Ephraim. "They say it, but they don't mean it. Intention there is not here and the heart is empty. Well, so what? Let it be so."

During most of the year the summerhouse was inhabited by only two people—Sarah, Aminadav's widow, and her father Ephraim. An Arab servant-woman from the neighboring village helped Sarah, and the Arab woman's husband came once or twice a week to care for the garden, to prune, to irrigate, and to rake.

Sarah drove her father firmly, because she wished his well-being. When he got very old Ephraim started to behave like a child and Sarah decided to tame him, so he would behave himself. He used to dirty his handkerchiefs, because he would blow his nose and spit into them without shame, and then fold them up again and lay them in his pocket. Sarah gave him paper tissues for the same purpose, and explained to him that cloth handkerchiefs were meant for wiping a little sweat off the forehead, whilst paper tissues could be dirtied and then thrown into the dustbin. But Ephraim said that all his life Bella-Yaffa had given him clean handkerchiefs and had allowed him to do with them as the spirit had moved him.

"Not Bella-Yaffa," Sarah corrected him, "but my mother, Rivka. But what do you think, that I am going to bend all day over the basin washing your filthy handkerchiefs? Here, take these, they're paper. That's modern and that's hygienic and that's good."

And when Ephraim continued to stand in his stubbornness and continued to filthy his handkerchiefs, Sarah took all his cloth handkerchiefs and hid them in a drawer concealed from the eye. All day long Ephraim searched for his handkerchiefs and toward evening he burst out crying and began to overturn all the drawers and cabinets in the house, casting their contents out onto the floor and emitting dirty words. Sarah was alarmed and called the Arab servant-woman and the two of them dragged him to his room and locked him behind lock and key and Sarah telephoned Jerusalem and told Oved that Grandfather was frisking about and was out of his mind. Oved told Rachel and the children heard and became alarmed. On Saturday the whole family drove out to the summerhouse to see what could be done.

When the Jerusalemites heard what had happened to Grandfather Ephraim, a flush of anger bloomed on Oved's cheeks. Disturbing memories surfaced and arose in his memory, connected not so much with himself as with his late brother Elyakum and what had happened between him and their mother long ago. But Oved knew how to restrain his fleeting emotions and explained to his mother that Grandfather Ephraim was no longer a child, and that it was too late to try to educate him. Oved did not believe that Ephraim was out of his mind, and it was much more likely that it was Sarah whose nerves had burst. If she wanted to, it was possible for her to go to Safed, to a rest home. In the meantime the Arab servant-woman could look after Grandfather Ephraim.

"You think I'll desert my father and leave him in the hands of an Arab woman?" screamed Sarah, offended, and ready, as she also said, to leave this house at once, with her father, and to go back to Tel Aviv.

Bella-Yaffa sat with Ephraim and caressed the back of his hand. "I'll give you some lovely handkerchiefs, as many as you want, Grandfather," Bella-Yaffa promised. And Ephraim shed a few tears and said to her in a whisper, "We two will run away from here one day and go to the settlement, and I will show you a new plantation which I planted this year, and I will teach you how to ride on horseback, and we will go out to the wadi together, until we find Bella-Yaffa."

"You've already found me," said Bella-Yaffa.

"Right," chuckled Ephraim, "but still we would be better off running away from here. There there are the new plantations and Na'aman is critically ill."

At the same time Uri, who had just finished the Gymnasium, explained to his mother Rachel and said:

"You should tell Grandmother Sarah two things. The first, that Grandfather Ephraim's days are numbered and if she does not want to have a bad conscience until the end of her life, she had better treat him nicely and patiently. Buy her fifty handkerchiefs and tell her there is no need to wash them, she can throw them into the dustbin. And the second thing, you can promise her that the time will come when she will be exactly like Grandfather Ephraim now, if not worse. And if she wants to be treated with respect, she should remember and pay attention."

"In my family we would never have reached such a situation," Rachel said to him. "Among us it is known how to respect elders."

"Very good for your family," said Uri. "But I'm a half-breed, half Ashkenazi and half Sephardi, right? So I'm telling you, if you don't speak with Grandmother Sarah, murder will happen here. And that is definitely not fitting for either of our families. Explain to her what a disgrace can happen here."

Murder there was none, and Ephraim lived about three years more and he died in his sleep and he was nearly ninety years old when he died. At his funeral no one wept, but everyone was present. Uri came home from the army, in officer's uniform; and Oved made the time to get away from his business immediately when he learned of Ephraim's death. Herzl, who was approaching sixty, stood to the side, as was his way, but this time he was quiet. He was the only one who guessed that among those accompanying there was one single soul that needed support, and so he pressed Bella-Yaffa to his body and embraced her shoulders, which were shivering, even though it was midsummer. When Ephraim's body was lowered into the grave, Bella-Yaffa turned her face and hid it on Herzl's chest and he stroked her hair but looked straight ahead, far beyond the people gathered there, and for the first time it happened to him that upon seeing his sister Sarah he did not remember the stable at all, and not his dead brother Aminadav and nothing else of all the things linked with the old house. All these were over and gone from his world and Bella-Yaffa was the only one who heard—and remembered all the days of her life—how Uncle Herzl muttered in English and said, "Goodbye, Daddy; farewell, see you soon."

A month later a third tombstone was erected, next to the tombstones of Aminadav and Elyakum. The inscription on Aminadav's tomb read: "A man of many deeds, a builder of the country, may he rest in peace." On the tombstone of Ephraim they wrote: "From the first of the courageous, pioneer of citrus-growing, layer of paths in the wilderness, let his soul remain forever in the memory of the bundle of the living." Whilst on the tombstone of Elyakum it was written: "Plucked off in the prime of his life."

"In the prime of his life," Uri wondered and giggled. "Why, he was thirty-four years old. It's just phraseology."

When Uri completed his military service the date was set for a party in the summerhouse, but then they had to postpone the party for ten days because in the meantime his Grandmother Sarah died all of a sudden, and she was sixty-four years old.

Many of Uri's comrades from his company came to the party. But apart from several words from his father's mouth, there were no speeches this time, but they ate and drank and told memories from their days as recruits. Bella-Yaffa did not take part in the celebration because she was bed-bound. She was sickly, and she was exempt from military service; and in the end she also had to interrupt her studies at the university, when a grievous weakness was discovered in her, with a low temperature. The doctor recommended an interruption of studies for one year, and he said that if she would spend this year in the summerhouse she would regain her health.

Bella-Yaffa did regain her health, more or less, but she did not go back to the university. In her bed she studied and read more in one year than she had absorbed in her three years of study in Jerusalem. When she got up on her feet and began to walk around the garden, she was already capable of reading Greek and Latin on her own, and from the poetry of England and France she knew countless pages by heart, but she recited them in the ears of not a man.

The Arab servant-woman now became a full member of the household at the summerhouse, because Bella-Yaffa wished not to return to Jerusalem. The husband of the Arab woman also came to live in the house, and from his mouth Bella-Yaffa learned the names of the weeds and flowers in the vicinity, and with his help she also improved her knowledge of the spoken Arabic language.

In the company of the Arab she would go out for day-long trips, on donkeyback, into the hills and the wadis in the environs of Wadi Millk, and from his mouth she used to write down many plant names and folk tales. And when the two of them became veritable friends, the Arab disclosed to her also that their summerhouse had come by a legend of its own. And this was the legend: The elders of the village Faradis used to tell that some generations ago a mysterious woman came in the night, indescribably beautiful, mounted on a horse, and in the night entered into the ruin, that very ruin where now festivities were arranged. A shepherd from the village had seen her when she came and his soul had almost departed from him out of fear. But the woman be-witched him and called him to come to her and enter into the ruin, and the bewitched shepherd followed her footsteps and was with her there all that night; and in the morning, when he rose to bid her farewell the woman had disappeared as if she had never been there. For fifty years passersby would hear a singing voice and a sighing voice emerging from the ruin and after another fifty years the skeleton of a woman was discovered under the heap of stones. And since then the singing voice and the sighing voice had stopped and had never again been heard in the world.

Bella-Yaffa wrote these things in her copybook and one day—she said to herself—she would compile all this folk material into one small volume, but not for publication. Yonas-Yehoshuah Bieberkraut would be permitted to read it; if he wished, he would write a preface.

One of Uri's uncles, the brother of his mother, had a business abroad, in women's garments and fashion accessories, and he had converted his name from Abraham Cordoviero to Abie Cordo, and once every year or two he would come to Israel for a visit. Upon arrival he would say that he had come for all the days of a month; but very soon he would telephone somewhere in Europe and announce that he had to return to his business immediately, because you cannot rely on the idiots. Immediately afterward he would telephone the police superintendent in Jerusalem and shout into the receiver, "I'm leaving, and you don't have to go on sending detectives after me and there is no need to bug my telephone calls." And the police superintendent, who was already acquainted with the matter, would reply that the surveillance was being called off.

A memorandum, sent by Mr. Cordo to the police superintendent several years ago, bore the following information:

Requiem for Na'aman

MEMORANDUM

For the attention of the Superintendent of the
Jerusalem Police.
Copies to the Minister of Justice and the Prime
Minister.

I, ABRAHAM CORDOVIERO, now known as Abie
Cordo, eighth generation in this country on my
father's side and second generation on my mother's
side, with the intention of putting an end to the
rumors and slanders that have been piled upon me
by various liars and villains, hereby declare that
everything written herein is complete truth.

On my father's side we belong to the family of
King David, and we had the proofs of this in
written documents and they were with me in my
flat, when I was married, and all these documents
were burnt in a fire when the burning was in the
above-mentioned flat, which was lit by Bibi
Turgeman, who was carrying on with my wife, as
you know from the trial that came to court after I
was attacked by a nervous attack and injured my
wife, until she died and departed from this world.

At that selfsame trial my family hired a lawyer,
and paid him a fortune so that he would plead that
I was mad, against my will and against the

truthful facts. And the judge, who also was a relative of my mother's, accepted this plea and I went for observation in a madhouse and I sat there for a while and was released.

And to this day I tell you that I was not mad. Because if I was mad, how is it that I went afterward to university and I studied and received a degree with distinction? How is it that a mad Jew gets a degree with distinction from the Gentiles, who are mostly anti-Semites?

And because of the above-mentioned reasons, and also a little bit because of my fear of the vengeance of my wife's brothers and several other people, I walked out of the country. And from that day on they talk about me and pronounce calumnies and conspire with the police and say about me that I am a spy for our enemies and work for foreign money. It's all sheer lies. There is only one truth, and these are the facts:

1. My money I made, I earned by my education, my talents, and my diligence.
2. I have no income from the enemy, only the income from my business in Paris, in London, and in Munich.
3. I have a lawyer, to whom all approaches should be referred, and he is Maître Busson, and everybody in Europe knows him.
4. I am not to be bothered when I come to the country for a goodwill visit.

Requiem for Na'aman

5. No transgressions have I transgressed and all
   my accounts are open to the proper authorities,
   through the above-mentioned Maître Busson.

   Summing up, I demand the protection of the
police. There is no reason to follow me or to bug
my telephone conversations or to pretend falsely
that I am not being persecuted at all.

   After having summed up the immediate
problems on the agenda, I will give something of
the general background: I am a Sephardi Jew, of
the purest Sephardi stock, and I saw in my
childhood the Ashkenazi Jews coming from all
over the world and grabbing positions and rudely
elbowing their way in and pushing us aside to the
corner. And all these newcomers have jargonesque
names like Rabinowitz and Schmendrikowitz. And
what do they do with their names? They change
them. Rabinowitz becomes Rabin and
Schmendrikowitz becomes Alouf. I said to myself:
If they rule over us, I'm in the Diaspora. And if
I'm in the Diaspora, I will change my name from a
Hebrew one to an outlandish one exactly the
opposite of what Rabinowitz does.

   That is the reason for the change of my name,
and that is one of the reasons for my departure to
the Diaspora.

   When will I return to the land of my
forefathers? This is a solemn oath, a saying of
honor and truth: When the Ashkenazis fold in

their rude elbows and become a minority. The day
Jerusalem has a police superintendent from our
people, and in the House of Parliament there will
be a Prime Minister of ours and in the army a
Chief of Staff of ours—then I shall know that no
danger is imminent for me, and I will return to my
father's house and to the motherland; as long as
she is occupied by you, I am waiting outside. And
from time to time I come to see, with my own
eyes, if there have been any changes.

> *Respectfully yours,*
> A. Cordo
> *An Israeli citizen, with*
> *foreign citizenship, according*
> *to the law.*

When Uri completed his service in the army, he went
to study law, like his father, but that same year he had
to interrupt his studies, because in 1956 another war
broke out, and the officers were called up to their units.
That was a short war, and yet, when Uri returned to his
studies, he found out that three in his class had fallen
in the war; about this Uri said, "Life is not an insur-
ance company, and if you want a State, you have to
pay the price. I remained alive just by chance but not
every day is Purim.* One day it's honey, another day

---

*A Jewish festival of merrymaking and drinking and mask-wear-
ing.

it's onion. You don't like it? Good-bye. There's nothing doing."

At the end of that year an unpleasant thing happened.

Uri decided that war was not a sufficient reason for losing a year of studies, and therefore he insisted on taking his examinations on the fixed date. His father told him it would be hard, and his mother said that nothing was burning and that he would not lose anything if he took another year at the university. But Uri relied on his talents, and to be sure he prepared for himself little slips which he tucked in various parts of his body and his clothes, and thus he reported to the examinations. And verily he would have almost passed all of them had he not been caught by an examiner, Professor Lindenbaum, *in flagrante*, when he drew out a slip and copied from it. Professor Lindenbaum thought it over, and for a moment was even inclined to disregard the matter entirely, because Uri was an intelligent student, an officer in the army who had been taken from his study bench and sent into war; and was it not a reason for forgiveness? But immediately he retracted, because the matter was indeed grave. Was not Uri about to become a lawyer, and in days to come might even become a judge in Israel; and if so—how could one forgive?

"Mr. Ben-Zion," said Professor Lindenbaum, "I regret to inform you that I am disqualifying your examinations and you will have to come back and be examined again next year."

Uri did not try to argue, but went to a lieutenant-colonel, an acquaintance of his father, told him what had

happened, and asked him to try and influence Lindenbaum.

"Explain to him," said Uri, "that I have good class
marks, and had it not been for the war, it's clear that I
would have passed the examinations without a hitch. So,
what, do I have to be punished for going to the army?
Are the evaders to receive diplomas while we eat shit?"

The lieutenant-colonel told another officer about it,
and much as it was unpleasant, they tried their luck and
telephoned Lindenbaum. They explained to him what
Uri had advised them to explain, and added an embel-
lishment of their own: "If you disqualify him, what it
means is that you are punishing an officer. What kind of
impression will that make in the army? Don't you understand that what is involved here is the morale of the
army? We have to encourage the youngsters to fulfill
their duty, not to deter them and to encourage evasion."

Old Lindenbaum heard and almost had a heart sei-
zure. He adamantly insisted upon his decision, and convened the Pedagogic Council.

Professor Kirsch said, "I cannot believe my ears."

Professor Bar-Nevo said, "If they insist, I suggest we
resign and notify the press."

Professor Bar-Zion said, "What is it? The days of
Dreyfus return and come again? Are the army and the
honor of the army to be more important than the truth?"

And Professor Elishevah Porat-Smirnovski said, "I
propose that we summon Uri Ben-Zion. That he report
here and tell us, to our faces, that he really wants us to

give him a diploma after he was caught copying. I want to hear what he has to say. There must be a personal confrontation here, if we actually want to understand what has happened to the Hebrew youth. We need to hear what this generation has to tell us. Perhaps our time has really come to retire? I request that Uri Ben-Zion be summoned to a meeting of the Pedagogic Council."

Uri heard about the invitation and was exultant.

"I'll teach them a lesson," he promised his mother and father. "I'll give them a beating with my tongue, if they're really prepared to listen."

Oved advised him to act with restraint, to express regret, and at the end concede and silence the whole matter. But Uri said, "Father, you can rely on me."

The whole day Uri sat in his room and prepared headings for his speech. This speech was supposed to be the first of many that Uri would make during his life, when he would be one of the jurists in Israel, a high-ranking officer in the reserves, and a manager of a contracting company which would build Israel's fortifications on the Suez Canal and in the Sinai Desert, when the day came.

And these are the words that the Professors Lindenbaum, Kirsch, Bar-Nevo, Bar-Zion, and Elishevah Porat-Smirnovski, members of the Pedagogic Council, heard from the youth Uri Ben-Zion, when he was almost twenty-two years old:

"Honored Professors, Madam and Gentlemen, it would seem that I stand here before you accused of only one accusation, the accusation of having copied in the examinations. To this accusation I would have confessed willingly and immediately. But you are actually affixing three charges upon me, and I refuse to confess to the second and the third. The second charge which you hurl at me is the fact that in the middle of my studies I left the university course in the law faculty and I went off to play football. Gentlemen, I did not go to play football. I went to fight the enemy. And not because I decided to do it, but because the government decided upon this. I could have claimed then: I'm studying. I'm a student, leave me alone. But I didn't say that, I stood up and went . . ."

"No one has blamed you for going to the army." Professor Lindenbaum tried to cut short his argument.

"Of course they have blamed me!" shouted Uri, raising his voice, "I have proof of it. You are punishing me, hence according to your opinion I have sinned. If I had not gone to the army, you wouldn't be punishing me, because I wouldn't have been forced to copy in the examinations. Do you really think I copied for fun, or for pleasure? I copied because I long to continue my studies and because as a result of the war I did not have time to prepare myself properly for the examination."

"I," said Professor Bar-Nevo, "because of this twisted logic alone, would disqualify you from becoming a jurist. You are standing here before us and making fun of us with a primitive exercise of sophistical speculation."

"That is debatable," said Uri calmly, "but I shall now turn to the third accusation, which is the gravest of all.

The third accusation which you are hurling against me is that I dare to dispute your very world outlook. And here, ladies and gentlemen, allow me to elaborate, so that there will be no misunderstandings. It was a great principle that our forefathers applied when they established: No decree may be enforced upon the public, unless the majority of the community can abide by it. Well then, Madam and Gentlemen, this principle has been forgotten from your hearts entirely. And not only from your hearts, you who are sitting here in this Pedagogic Council, but this principle has not even been taken into account by the entire generation which you represent. In fact, this is the failure of Zionism in its entirety."

"Just a moment, just a moment," called Professor Elishevah Porat-Smirnovski. "Honored colleagues, my only request is that this be recorded in the protocol word for word. Please continue, Mr. Ben-Zion."

"Please," said Uri, "I shall speak very slowly, so that everything can be written down. So, good Jews thought that something should be done for the Jewish people. Miserable, degraded, and persecuted. Just look at them and see how they appear: pale, not suntanned, bent over, thin, involved in all kinds of speculation and matchmaking, and how all beat and spit upon them. And unjustly, for just look what a wonderful people they are in fact: they have Professor Einstein . . ."

"Professor Einstein was forty years later," Professor Lindenbaum, not restraining himself, called from his place.

"All right then, not Einstein. So Maimonides," Uri
agreed. "Maimonides, I understand, was before the Ka-
towitz Conference.* So, the Jews have plenty of ge-
niuses, and also ordinary highly gifted people and
Rothschilds and all kinds of violinists and pianists and
what not. Therefore it is not just to treat them shame-
fully. This whole wheel has to be reversed. If until now
we have been pale, now we shall be suntanned like Bedouins, and if until now we have been bent over, so from
now on we shall walk so erect that it shall be with difficulty that we will prevent ourselves from falling backward. And if until now we have been parasites, so from
now on there will be such productivity that Stakhanov †
will look like a dog in comparison. And if until now we
have been forced to cheat a little bit, to bargain, to be a
bit cunning, then from now on we will be exceedingly
righteous.

"And now I am coming to my main point. Upon this
people, who are now known as citizens of the State of
Israel, a decree has been decreed with which the majority is incapable of conforming. It's impossible for a whole
nation to be righteous and holy. There is no such thing.
We are only flesh and blood. A little crack has to be left
for small sins. If no such crack is left, then the pressure
is too great, nearly bursting. Even in the wheel of a car

---

*The first political Zionist meeting, before official Zionism ex-
isted.

†A paragon of productivity in Stalinist Russia.

there is a small valve, and in every steam engine too. When there is too much pressure, the valve opens and some air comes out. That's no disaster. But you, gentlemen, have left no such crack. The demands are absolute: a light unto the Gentiles, for out of Zion shall go forth the law; the kibbutzim must serve as a model to all the socialists and communists in the world; in the Weizmann Institute they are about to prove that they can produce petroleum from oranges, because if we don't come up with some astounding invention, that would be a sign that we have failed. And each Israeli citizen has to be a kind of miniature Moses. Madam and Gentlemen, from this business there will be only trouble. A human being is ninety percent water and the rest is organic matter, which decomposes into minerals and metals. Let him live according to the laws by which he was created. Do not overload this animal with more than he can carry. And I tell you that it will run amok. Instead of righteous people we shall have a State full of petty violators of the law. And after that big violators of the law and finally real criminals. And why am I saying all this? Where is the connection with the matter for which I was called here? Well, the connection is very simple: don't press. Start at once to legislate a law in the university, according to which each student who has to go to the army in the middle of a term will receive certain concessions in examinations, that special consideration will be given to him and to the sacrifice that he has been forced to make.

"And if you, the professors, do this, then the government and the Parliament too will learn from you. And when they come to legislate laws they will remember that we have become sufficiently suntanned and sufficiently erect and have pretended long enough to be righteous and supremely saintly. Now the time has come to be human beings a little bit. From this rostrum I warn and decree: If you continue to walk with your head against the wall, if you pretend that the nation of Israel is destined for such a kind of fate and role and destiny that no other nation has ever succeeded in realizing, then this whole business will be dismantled. I can already hear the creakings and the sounds of the avalanche. I have concluded."

The chairwoman, Professor Porat-Smirnovski, asked the members of the Council if any of them had anything to say, but they kept silent and shrugged their shoulders.

"That will be enough, Mr. Ben-Zion," said Professor Porat-Smirnovski. "You may go."

"Just one question, please," said Professor Lindenbaum. "Those things you said here, from where did they come to you? That is to say, are they the domain of many of your age group, or did you ponder them yourself?"

"I learned them at home," said Uri. "My father is a lawyer and a lot of dirt flows through his office."

Professor Porat-Smirnovski told her husband, an engineer in the electricity company, and Professor Bar-Nevo told his brother, a Member of Parliament, and Bar-Zion told his wife, a teacher in the Gymnasium, and Lindenbaum lugged and brought the matter to the atten-

tion of the Minister of Education. Somehow the story
rolled to the papers and one newspaper published a leading article, contending that we must listen deeply to
these voices now bursting forth from among the youth.
"The inherent danger," wrote the newspaper, "is that a
generation will grow up here which verily will excel in
the battlefield, but in the end of the day will not know
what it is fighting for."

In one newspaper it was written that copying in examinations is a well-known phenomenon in every edu-
cational institution, and those who copy should be
treated with the gravest severity. "No sophistry and no
ideological argument, as it were," wrote that newspaper,
"can or should be allowed to dim the judgment of the
university authorities. To surrender to such arguments
as those raised by the student Abner Etzioni is to open a
door for the destruction of the academic framework. On
the other hand, there is more than a nucleus of sense in
his other argumentations, although this is neither the
time nor the place to treat them."

Uri went back to his studies and finally he finished
with distinction and received his diploma. In 1959 he
joined his father's firm and that same year began studying business administration in evening courses.

In the summerhouse lived Bella-Yaffa all the days of
the year, and her parents asked themselves if she was
ever likely to emerge from there and come out into the
wide world. Twenty-three years of age she was, sickly

but remarkably beautiful, and she showed no sign of affinity with any man among the few men that she had met. Her one and only friend was that clumsy elderly man who had made those gathered at the festivities held in honor of the late Grandfather Ephraim laugh. The age of Yonas-Yehoshuah Bieberkraut was nearly twice the age of Bella-Yaffa, and therefore nothing was in fact found amiss in the visits he frequently made to the summerhouse. After all, Bieberkraut was her teacher, not her suitor.

Bieberkraut used to come on Friday afternoons and bring with him textbooks in the German language, volumes of poetry which had been printed abroad, and also literary magazines from the world press. He had a room of his own in the summerhouse, and there the Arab servant-woman would bring his breakfast, because he was an early riser, whilst Bella-Yaffa remained late in bed, because most of the night she occupied herself with reading and translating. In the early morning Bieberkraut would go out alone for a stroll and come back at the time when Bella-Yaffa was ready to sit down to her German lessons. In the afternoon they would listen together to records and in the evening—but not always—Bella-Yaffa would allow him to glance at a translation she had done, or at the collection of folk tales she had scribbled down from the mouth of her Arab friend. Only very rarely did she put into his hand a slip of paper on which was written a poem she had composed; but then she would hastily leave the room and leave him alone, and sometimes would not return at all, and they would see each other again the next morning, and never exchange a single word about that poem. But when Bieberkraut would travel away on Sunday mornings, he would leave in his room a sealed envelope, for Bella-Yaffa, and in that envelope there was a letter in which he expressed his opinion.

The parents and the brother of Bella-Yaffa were, all in all, quite satisfied with this situation. The presence of this strangely behaved daughter in their big house in Jerusalem always swarming with guests would have embarrassed them and might even have given the family a bad name. But on the other hand, both the parents and the brother cherished not only a familial affection for Bella-Yaffa, but even some kind of hidden admiration. Every one of them felt in his own way that this daughter was accomplishing something important which each of them had neglected or lost somewhere. To the members of the family it was not so clear what this thing was, but Uri managed to define something of it: "Sometimes my mad sister poses a certain question mark upon the sanity of us all. I, for example, don't know exactly what I'm pursuing in life. And how is it with you, Father? Do you know? But Bella-Yaffa, it seems to me that she knows. Or does it only seem to me?"

Uri could not have known that in that same week his sister had put into Bieberkraut's hands a slip of paper, on which it was written:

> Whither do they run, all my blue days?
> Whither—all the days of grayness?
> In the garden long withered the brambles

Lo!—theirs no memory of bitterness!
The roses have bowed down their heads also
And their pinkness long ago turned crimson.
Not only I. Perhaps they too
Are thinking about you, Na'aman.

The next day Bieberkraut scribbled, inside his sealed envelope, "Who is Na'aman?"

Never before had he asked questions and Bella-Yaffa was embarrassed, until the idea came to her to lay a sealed envelope of her own on Bieberkraut's table, and when he came next week he would receive an answer, but they would never raise the subject in their conversation. And thus Bella-Yaffa wrote in her first letter to Yonas-Yehoshuah Bieberkraut:

Dear Friend, I don't know who Na'aman is. I can only surmise and guess. My great-grandfather told me about him when I was a little girl. Perhaps he is a kind of Putois from Anatole France's story. A creature who never existed, but lives in people's imaginations, because they had need of him and therefore they invented him. It was not I who invented Na'aman, but my great-grandfather. Or perhaps Na'aman was not an invention, but flesh and blood. This is something I will never know nor does it make any difference.

And now that you know that Na'aman may never have existed at all, I can tell you who Na'aman is. But first I have to preface it and tell

you who I am. You know that my name is Bella-
Yaffa, but you don't know how this name came
into the world. It was the name of my great-
grandfather's first wife, and when I was born he
insisted that they call me by her name.
Fortunately it turned out that my mother had an
aunt whose name was Bella and it was only for this
reason that my mother's family agreed to my
great-grandfather's suggestion. My mother takes
care to call me Bella; and when someone calls me
Bella-Yaffa, she wrinkles up her nose. And here I
have a feeling that Na'aman is somehow connected
with that Bella-Yaffa. Perhaps Na'aman was that
man to whom she ran away, when she left my
great-grandfather. Thus, at any rate, I heard from
my mother. All this happened—as in the legends
—fifty years ago, or perhaps a hundred and fifty.
And if so, Na'aman walked upon the face of this
earth many years ago, and one day he decided to
reject all that the earth offers to its inhabitants and
he dived under the water. I can imagine how it
happened. He was in love with the stars, but they
were far away, and then he fell in love with the
flowers and the grasses, but they withered and
died in the summer and Na'aman thought that
they had betrayed him. Is it not that we all feel
angry and offended when the beloved soul departs
from us, even if it goes the way of all flesh?
Na'aman wanted therefore to go to the place where

the roots of the flowers meet the stars, when they are reflected in water. So he dived. But he did not stop singing and making music. My great-grandfather told me that Na'aman plays music under the water and that his hair floats and moves on the surface of the stream. And it is possible that all of us have seen his hair and we mistakenly thought that it was water weeds, thin and gentle. Verily we never know what it is that we see. And I envy Na'aman, because he had the strength to reject all the earthly offerings, and I do not have that kind of strength, I am captive in a prison from which the youth Na'aman broke out. That is all I know about him, and in my poems I try to tell him that I know.

Some time after these things Yonas-Yehoshuah Bie-berkraut told Bella-Yaffa that he intended to devote the rest of his life to a certain literary project; if it were not tackled immediately, however, we might miss the oppor-tunity. It would be some kind of dictionary arranged alphabetically, into which would be assembled all the nouns in the Bible and the Talmud: the names of imple-ments, objects, plants, and agricultural tools also. The purpose of this dictionary would be to strive to come closer to the true identification of the objects named by these nouns, in order to establish the connection between the new State and the ancient past of our nation upon a solid basis of clear knowledge.

"I'll give you an example," said Bieberkraut. "This vegetable which is called in German *Gurke*, and in English *cucumber*, we have called by the Hebrew name *melafefon*. Why we have done that I do not know. But clearly there is a complete mistake here. *Melafefon* is what in Arabic is called *malfuf*, which we mistakenly call *kruv* in Hebrew, and the English call *cabbage*. *Malfuf* because it consists of rolls of leaves, *lifuf* being the term for rolling. And *kruv*, the word which has come into English as *cherub*, was apparently the name of an angel, not a vegetable. And why is this process so dangerous? Because lack of knowledge engenders disruption, and disruption proceeds to alienation, and at the end of this process not only will our spiritual culture disintegrate, but also our material culture, and in the end we will disappear and be erased from the face of the earth."

"And how do you intend to arrive at the truth?" said Bella-Yaffa. "Is it possible to summon our ancient forefathers from their graves and ask them to identify for our sake the nouns the meanings of which have been lost to us?"

"It is to this very project that I want to devote my life," cried Bieberkraut triumphantly. "You have understood what many and good people have not even guessed. Verily, verily, I hope to divine by the familial spirit. And I have with me the tools for such a purpose, because I communicate with several languages and I am acquainted with the sources. It will be hard work, and you, my friend, will be able to help me, because you have a discriminating ear and a sensible heart and you know Greek, not to mention other languages."

In 1960 Bieberkraut brought his articles and his library to the summerhouse and Bella-Yaffa told her parents that both of them would live on what had been allotted to her alone, and that Bieberkraut also had a little money from his early pension, as he had retired from teaching. Oved and Rachel looked at each other, and Oved said, "Can you imagine if all this would have happened here, in Jerusalem, for all the world to see?"

And Rachel said, "That comes from your family, not from mine. Among us there are none like those."

During the next fourteen years Bieberkraut and Bella-Yaffa were to labor on their dictionary, and it is known that in the year 1974 they had reached the letter *B*.

24.

WHEN OVED BEN-ZION took Rachel Cordoviero to wife in the early Thirties of this century, there was in his deed something of an innovation. There had not been many cases of marriage between the Sephardis and Ashkenazis. Indeed, such things had happened, and even during the days of the Turks it happened that Ashkenazi men and Ashkenazi women had married Sephardi Jews, but in those days the Ashkenazis had become assimilated among the Sephardis because the latter were the élite of

Jewish society in the Land of Israel. Later on the Ashkenazis became more numerous in the Land of Israel and highhandedly stamped their mark: Yiddish became the market language and in the schools they taught poems which had been written in Odessa and books which had been translated from Yiddish. And even when they taught the poems of the poet Yehudah Halevi, no one would have imagined that Yehudah Halevi had been a *frenk,** not an Ashkenazi. And Maimonides definitely was imprinted upon the imaginations of pupils as a diligent *yeshivah†* scholar from Volozhyn or Vilna.

Proud and insulted, the Sephardi Jews preserved in their hearts a sense of superiority, together with the feeling of deprivation which over the course of years etched yet another groove in the nation. The borderlines passed therefore not only between citizens and workers, but also between Ashkenazis and non-Ashkenazis.

The entry of Oved into the closed house of the Cordoviero family—a house which had preserved ancient patriarchal manners and stylized aristocratic habits—was accompanied by a turning up of noses and a kind of protest from some of the brothers and cousins of Rachel. They consoled themselves in the fact that he was a descendant of the first pioneers, and was not one of the newcomers from Poland. Nor did it escape their notice that he was the son of a rich industrialist, and that he

*That is, a Sephardi Jew.

† Religious seminary.

had a lawyer's title. Nevertheless, what was he looking for among the Sephardis? What had caused him to choose their sister? If he had been a son of the poor, they would have rejected him totally; but since he was not a son of the poor, why did he choose to match himself with those who were not of his kind?

"You should know," one of Rachel's brothers said to him, "my sister is not going to make you *gefilte* fish. You can forget about that, my dear. Among us you'll eat fish with *hreimeh*,* until your belly burns up."

Oved understood what was said to him, and why they spoke to him the way they spoke, and he never forgave them for having done so. His relations with the Cordoviero tribe were imbued with continuous politeness and niceties, but apart from partnerships these relations were never developed to the level of friendship. But not so the relations of Uri with his many uncles and cousins, who were named Valero, Matalon, Mani, and Sassoon. They accepted Uri as if he were one of them, since Rachel's blood flowed in his veins and it is known that a man is the son of his mother and not of his father.

Grandfather Cordoviero used to stroke his head with affection, when he would introduce him to his acquaintances, and would say, "Blessed be he by God, my grandson. Look at him and see, you would never be able to tell that there was some Rabinowitz in their family."

"Abramson," Uri used to correct him. "Why Rabinowitz all of a sudden?"

---

*A North African word for an extremely hot, burning spice.

Requiem for Na'aman

"I was only speaking figuratively," laughed Grand-father Cordoviero. "How can I distinguish among their names? They're all in jargon."

About a year after Uri started to work in his father's firm he founded a company for the production of prefab-ricated building units, in partnership with one of his cousins. His father got him a contract with the Defense Ministry and about two years later Uri left his father's firm and went to live in Tel Aviv. The house which had belonged to his grandfather and grandmother, Aminadav and Sarah, was still standing in its place in Rothschild Boulevard, and both of its floors were let to tenants. Uri insisted upon living in a street which by then had fallen from its importance, and cleared one floor for himself. And later on he managed to clear the second floor too. There was not much commercial rationale in this, but he was drawn to do what he did because he felt that a duty was incumbent upon him to preserve the heritage of his forefathers. When he was asked why he insisted upon wasting money on an old building in a district that was rapidly becoming abandoned—when everyone who could was moving toward the north, toward the new quarters of the town—he said that one should not aban-don the battlefield, and that he would restore to Roths-child Boulevard the glory of its past. The Cordoviero family praised him for this, and when he heard the praise of him from their mouths, he felt that he had acted ac-cording to an imperative which came to him from the Sephardi part of his blood: one must prefer the old to the new, and adherence to tradition endows the one who husbands tradition with a power which is not to be found in the hands of those running after innovations and external glitter.

The Ashkenazi side of his blood led Uri to renovate the old house, both inside and outside, until in every respect it resembled those modern houses in north Tel Aviv. Now the house stood in Rothschild Boulevard like a gold tooth in a rotten mouth with uprooted teeth. Soon after there were found people like him who renovated their houses, and of all that glory of the old and dreaming Tel Aviv, nothing remained but the name of the street and several little lanes leading to it, where to this day there remain houses in which the sandstone peeps out from under the peeling plaster.

On the ground floor of the house Uri located his of-fices, which now included a law firm with a partner and also the offices of the company producing the prefabri-cated building units, which was in partnership with his cousin. On the upper floor Uri lived alone in four rooms, the immense dimensions of which remained from the old structure.

Before he turned thirty years old he already had a mature expression on his face, older than his age, and people much older than him saw no difficulty in discuss-ing business matters with him in complete confidence, as if he belonged to the previous generation. At the same time people of his own age easily found him a companion in the amusement of the kind that wealthy bachelors indulge in. And Uri treated both these and those equally with a fine and precise measure of distance, which had a greater force of attraction than hint of rejection. It could be said that he had no friends at all, apart from the single and special connection which formed between himself and his grandfather's stepbrother, that is, uncle Herzl.

From his ancient bungalow on the family estate, in the southern settlement which was now like a kind of museum of the early settlers, Herzl went on conducting the orchard business which he had inherited from his father Ephraim. Around the ancient family house popped up various white buildings, elongated and low, and Herzl heard that this was a sanatorium for tuberculosis, but he never set foot there ever.

And it happened that one day Herzl had to go to Tel Aviv, to a meeting of the Citrus Fruit Marketing Council. He completed his business late in the afternoon and thought of going back home, when he suddenly remembered that the grandson of his brother and sister, Aminadav and Sarah, had settled in Tel Aviv and had gone to live in the house where Herzl himself had stayed about seventeen years earlier when his brother had died and he had had to take care of the consolidation of the affairs of the deceased. Herzl therefore looked for and found the name of Uri Ben-Zion in the telephone book and said to him, "How would you like to come and have supper with me this evening in the hotel?"

Uri immediately invited him to come to the house on Rothschild Boulevard and promised him that his housekeeper would prepare dishes so marvelous that no chef in any hotel would be capable of competing with them. And so it happened that Herzl, aged sixty-three, and Uri, who was not yet thirty, made a surprising discovery which can be epitomized in one sentence: There is no difference between the loneliness of a man aged sixty-three and the loneliness of a man whose future is to be lonely all his days, even though he does not know it yet.

Although it was not their first meeting, it became clear to Uri—as soon as he saw Herzl Abramson entering the house—that the real owner of this house was now stepping on its threshold, and that one word from the master of the house would be sufficient for Uri to feel that he had to pack his effects and vacate the place. And at the same time Herzl breathed freely when he realized that indeed he did not make a mistake, and that Uri was, at long last, the only being in the whole family to whom he might get accustomed and maybe like. After Elyakum's death Herzl had believed that in the family no memory remained of people bearing a dream and with a heart.

The height of Herzl's stature, his bony leanness, his elegant attire and his white mustache completely captured Uri's imagination, and he imagined what a marvelous and impressive companion Herzl could be if Uri were to appear in his company among businessmen or even among his young friends, the partners of his amusements. The restrained speech, the silence of his smiles, his ability to listen, with a tilt of his head, the pipe in his mouth, were like a message from a strange world, a world that had sunk and about which old men told stories.

Uri's dining room was filled all of a sudden with outlandish odors, the smell of those places from which come the elegant cars, the expensive tableware, the tourists who are seen in the lobbies of the hotels in Tel Aviv. Here sits a man, a member of the family, the brother of Grandfather Aminadav, and he does not resemble anyone else in the family. He was really what Uri was hoping to become, when he grew old.

Uri was very careful with his words; and when Herzl asked him about his affairs, Uri did not brag a lot, but minimized his achievements, speaking lightly about his humble endeavors, and about his plans.

When supper was over he urges Herzl to spend the night in his house, and leads him to the room intended for guests, and he says, "If you permit me, let this be your room from now on, whenever you want to come. Please accept the offer. This is a request."

Herzl draws the pipe out of his mouth, nods slightly to thank him, but does not say a word. He only smiles. Why then has he taken the pipe out of his mouth?—Uri asks himself and answers himself: Apparently because that is the thing to do. It's a small charm, which also has to be studied.

When Uri turned thirty he arranged a party to which he invited several beauties in the company of whom he and his friends of his own age used to amuse themselves, but the men at the party were all old, businessmen, whom he took care to meet in complete separation from his nightlife. Herzl was the guest of honor, and was honored with toasting the health of the celebrant.

"To the health of my brother's grandson, Lieutenant Uri Ben-Zion," said Herzl, sipped from his glass, and sat down at his place. Every one of those who were present gave his own interpretation to the odd content of the short toast. Some saw in it a right-wing militaristic caprice, and some saw it as an expression of the pride of the old generation in the achievements of the State and the change that had occurred in the scale of values of the society. Uri alone dimly surmised that the toast implied a certain reprimand, and when the guests dispersed and Herzl remained behind to stay for a night's sleep, Uri said, "Why all of a sudden Lieutenant?"

Herzl relaxed in his armchair and answered calmly:

"The situation is becoming very severe, Uri, and I am sure that you feel it in your business. What you don't realize, perhaps, is that very soon the situation will become more severe and you are liable to lose everything you have built up. I think it's almost certain. All your affairs are bound up with a very thin upper layer of the economy, in commerce and building. You have no roots in agriculture, and I suggest you stop to consider this. There are going to be wars here. And if not wars, then incessant skirmishes. The army is gradually becoming the true ruler of the State. So why should you lag behind? Why should you be just a lieutenant? Before you stretch lean and very bad years for business. Enlist in the army in the meantime and rise in rank. When you come out of there, you will have in your hands ties with the help of which you will be able to go on from where you left off, and with greater success. Think about it, Uri, you have to become at least lieutenant-colonel. In our family there has to be a lieutenant-colonel."

"There are two lieutenant-colonels in my mother's family," said Uri.

"In *our* family, I said," remarked Herzl pedantically.

That night, in 1965, Uri did not close an eye. In his mind he reviewed the complicated arrangements that would enable him to freeze, at least partially, the activities of the law firm and the building company, with his partners carrying the burden and saving what could be saved, until after the storm. In the morning the plan was clear enough and within two months he enlisted in the standing army and on that occasion was received within the rank of captain.

In 1966 things reached such a low ebb as was not known before, and some twenty thousand people fled in panic and went to Canada and the United States. In the summer of 1967 the enemy moved his armies toward the borders of the Negev. In the family circles they spoke of a siege and of a ghetto, of the threshold of extinction and of the beginning of the end. What was said at the General Staff headquarters of the army, and at Cabinet meetings, was not clear and was not known. No one understood why the war had not already broken out.

In the middle of the summer the decision fell at long last and the first shot was fired. Within two days the air force of the enemy was destroyed and within a week the army of the conquerors stood upon occupied territory. By the end of the year Uri was released from the army, with the rank of lieutenant-colonel, and Grandfather Cordoviero said, "A third general in our family. Show me even one in the Rabinowitzes."

From the Cordoviero tribe no one fell in the war this time and among the Ben-Zions and Abramsons there were no more soldiers, apart from Uri. Oved was aged fifty-four when the war broke out, and when he came to offer his services to the army, they sent him home with a smile and a slap on the shoulder. But the junior partner in Uri's law firm was killed and his secretary's brother came out with severe burns which deformed his body irreparably. It was a war which the professionals and the world press described as a clean war, short and to the point; the Israelis had lost about eight hundred and fifty men. He who had no victim in his family desired to go dancing. Suddenly it became clear that the empty coffers of the State were rapidly filling up, and that money was starting to stream in from abroad and from the Jewish Diaspora. The whole West Bank of the Jordan had been occupied and the Old City of Jerusalem was filled with holiday-makers, who swarmed upon the small shops and the niches of Arab restaurants. And within one week scores of millions of pounds were spent there.

The Arabs in the occupied territories were so stunned

that for several months they would smile at the Israeli conquerors, as if they were an army of salvation and a population of brothers, who had returned and met again after a prolonged separation. Only after about half a year did the Arabs shake off the shock and here and there begin laying mines or bombs, or hurling a grenade.

And the Israelis, who when they went out to this war meant all in all to shake off from themselves a frightening threat, gradually began to change their minds, until only a few months later they believed wholeheartedly that this war had originally been meant to liberate the landscapes of the Bible, and to return to the bosom of the motherland the stones of the Wailing Wall. All of a sudden the number of repenters increased astonishingly and in the newspapers you could hear the voices of people who had found the Jewish faith alive in their hearts again. Here and there a senior officer, whilst he was lecturing about the war, told the story of how he had come to realize, at a moment of fatal danger, that Divine Providence has turned Its eye upon us for good.

Finally, there was in the nation almost entire agreement about one thing, which was beyond dispute and beyond differences of opinion and views. And this agreement was called by the name of *miracle*. All agreed to believe that a miracle had been made for us, one of those miracles that the Holy Blessed One had performed for our forefathers in every generation when the wicked ones had set upon us to destroy us. This entire agreement did not come into the world because anyone wanted to undermine, God forbid, the achievements of the army, but because such an agreement created an atmosphere that was comforting to everyone. The religious found in the miracle a reinforcement of their point of view; those in power found the atmosphere of miracle convenient for robbing the alms money, the donations, the investments and the allowances and the loans, that now streamed into the State in overwhelming strength. Is it not that in an hour of miracle one does not pay attention to minutiae and one does not go into details, but breaks loose in merrymaking, as befits miracles?

It is known that since the day of the destruction of the Temple, prophecy was taken away from prophets and given to the deaf, the fool, and the suckling. And that is why most people were wary about donning the mantle of prophets. But the number of those who pretended to be dreamers of dreams and seers of visions, on a humble scale, now became great and exceedingly immense. There were those who said, "I knew, I always knew, that already in my days such a thing would come to pass." And others said, "Only a blind man and a fool did not sense and did not feel that this victory had to take place in these very days."

This belief became common currency, and if it was difficult for several proclaimed atheists to change their minds all of a sudden and become real believers, it was easy even for such as them to believe in the eternity of Israel, at least, or in the historical imperative, or in the Jewish Man, as a minimal program.

And the moment that this divine consciousness pene-

trated the brains of those repenters, they hastened to
cover the upper parts of their brains with a small *kipa*
cap, so that it would place a partition between them and
the sky, lest they notice up there that until then this
brain had been empty of faith.

Hundreds of thousands of the Children of Israel
would set out every Saturday morning to the new territories, and roamed in cars and on foot, and entered into
Hebron, into Nablus, into Jenin, and into Tul Karem,
and some reached the most remote villages, beyond clefts
of the rocks, such as Artas beyond the Pools of Solomon,
which is the biblical Seif Selah Etam. Lovers of archae-
ology, as numerous in our places as the number of families, would buy from the villagers potsherds and plates,
jars and statuettes, all the things the villagers had robbed
from the numerous excavations. Lovers of art would buy
Greek icons from Bethlehem dealers and the women
would buy embroidered dresses of *fellahin* women and
would wear them in their homes, when receiving guests,
as a kind of evening dress. Women who were not endowed with culture and imagination would swarm upon
the vegetable stalls in the markets and buy vegetables at
less than half our market price.

From time to time a mean Arab would shoot at this
gay bunch of holiday-makers, and then the journeys
would stop for a week, until the army would purify the
area; and within a week the stream to the territories was
renewed, because there is no stopping multitudes who
woke up all of a sudden one morning and saw that they
are a great nation in a great country, treading on the soil

of their forefathers and cuddling their past. All the more so when the vegetables are so cheap, and Tel Aviv is so boring.

And in this huge and immense crowd Herzl Abramson's place was not left out. Seventy years of age was the man, thin and agile, and the years had not left their mark on him, apart from his mustache that was white and the hair of his head that had turned gray. Every Saturday he would go in his car, alone, and would sail into places he had known as a child and a youth, places where he had sojourned in the days before 1948. From that year on the country had been divided into a zone occupied by the Jews and a zone occupied by the enemy; and unfortunately the enemy had held those very places that Herzl loved so much. Now, with the roads opened and the borders canceled, he returned to his childhood estate and traveled backward in time, just as it is told in science-fiction books. Who could equal him and who would resemble him? Toward old age he found renewed pleasure, and again he returned and refreshed his use of the Arabic language which was on his lips, and would enter into conversations with men sitting in the coffeehouses of the villages, listening to and telling Arabic legends and parables, which were partly primitive wisdom and partly obscenities. And into the ears of the Arabs he did not hesitate to give vent to his language, because as a child he had been accustomed to that, and now he saw that the restraint for nineteen years had been very difficult.

Toward night he would come back home, tired and

happy, whilst in his car there were wrapped parcels containing sticky honey cakes, mutton, coffee ground with cardamom, and some thin *pittas*, of the kind called *tzalouf*, which the Jews cannot prepare unless they are Yemenites. But alas, the Yemenites in Israel have now accustomed themselves to eat *kümmel* bread.

Herzl did not stop making these journeys until the day of his death, in 1974, at the age of seventy-seven. Every Saturday, without depriving himself of even one week, he would go to the West Bank or to the Old City of Jerusalem, and every week he discovered that the power of renewal does not melt with time; on the contrary, it increases and mounts.

"If, God forbid, we'll have to return the territories to the enemy," said Herzl to Uri, "I know what I'm going to do. I'll become a Moslem and go to live over there."

"First of all, we won't return them," Uri said. "And secondly, you won't become a Moslem."

"Oh yes I will become a Moslem, in protest," explained Herzl. "If this government returns the territories, I don't want to be a Jew."

Uri did not take part in the big celebrations because he was too preoccupied. The rehabilitation of his law firm was not difficult, but the building company demanded a change of dimensions. If Uri had continued on the same scale as before the war, he would not have been able to join in the possibilities now opening up. First of all—building for the civilians; but most of all—building for the army. And the fortifications in Sinai, and the work in harbors, in Ashdod and in Eilat, and the containers, and the pipes, and the drilling, and the housing projects, and the roads, and the airfields. And what should he invest in? And how should he register the companies? And how should he arrange income tax? To cheat is out of the question. But also it is not necessary to be a fool. But all this devours time, and in the meanwhile someone else grabs a piece of the cake; and it's a pity. He had the connections to grasp almost every available piece, but if you are not alert, you don't see what there is in the field. And a man has only one pair of eyes, and one pair of hands. You can go mad. But you don't complain.

There were several short intermissions in Uri's activities, like the sudden death of Grandfather Cordoviero, and his funeral, and like the illness of his sister Bella-Yaffa, who all of a sudden had to be hospitalized in a sanatorium for nervous illnesses. Bieberkraut, the fool, saw fit to telephone Uri of all people about this; could he not have called Oved and Rachel? However, Uri did not evade his duty, and within about half a week succeeded in finding a good place for his sister and also in taking care that the whole matter would be kept secret. And immediately he returned to work.

To parties and restaurants he would go only if he was sure that among those present there would be people with whom it is worthwhile or necessary to be in contact. For sheer pleasure he had no time, but each year he would promise himself that next year he would take a holiday and go on an extended trip to Europe or America in the company of one of the beauties. He did not know that he would indeed go there, not on a holiday trip but in fact for business affairs, and not in the company of one of the beauties but in the company of one of his partners, and not for an extended journey, but for three or four days, and not once but almost every two or three months in the years between 1968 and 1973.

With great toil these five years passed and flew by, but when he looked back on them, it seemed to him that only yesterday had he been released from the army. Apart from the money he accumulated during these years, and the number of companies he founded and disbanded and assembled anew, nothing happened, apart from the promises which he made himself, and which he always postponed.

But in the midst of all this he did keep up one tradition after all, which was part of the spirit of the time, and took care to observe it zealously: he never gave up the Sabbath Eve dinner every week. As he was a bachelor, and also much liked and wanted among his acquaintances, the wives of his friends with whom he had served in the army or was a partner in business would invite him to the family table on Friday evening. On most occasions he would go to homes in the officers' quarter or in Ramat Aviv and Neve Avivim, which are near Tel Aviv.

Less than a year after the end of the war, at the beginning of 1968, a plane landed at Lydda and out of it came Uncle Abraham Cordoviero, alias Abie Cordo. Immediately after he passed through the passport inspection he went to a telephone booth and rang the police superintendent in Jerusalem.

"Surely you knew that I am arriving today. I want you to know that I protest most vigorously against the cruel treatment you have cruelly treated me with and I demand that it stop at once."

The police superintendent told him that he would give appropriate instructions. Then Abie Cordo drove to the house of his ancestors in Jerusalem, prostrated himself upon his father's grave, and on that occasion swore to avenge his death. After that he notified his sister Rachel and her husband Oved to vacate a room for him for several months, because this time he had come to pluck the fruits of victory. He hired a car and would descend to Tel Aviv two or three times a week and he likewise frequently visited the chambers of bank managers and asked for loans.

After several weeks of mysterious comings and goings Uncle Abie Cordo came to Uri with a vigorous demand that Uri gather in his house in Tel Aviv some of his very close friends.

"But only those who are influential or have connections with the influential institutions," Uncle Cordo explained. "People who have brains, energy, and a strong standing in society."

"Why?" Uri wanted to know.

"Don't ask and do what I tell you. You won't regret it. They'll hear from me such things that will alter the course of life."

"The course of life is good even without your advice," said Uri.

"And it'll be even better with my advice," said Uncle Cordo.

And thus on a wintry Saturday evening in the year 1968 there arrived at Uri's house seven men of stature and renown—Arik Ron, Ronni Ronnen, Nuri Yaron, Ron Oren, Oren Laron, Uri Renan, and Arnon Shmuel-sohn.

This last one was the only one who had not changed his name into Hebrew, because his father had taken care of that in his will. All the others had activated their imaginations on an early rung of the national revival, and had chosen distinctive and different names, each one according to his heart's desire and according to the counsel of bookish friends and people who knew the language.

So they gathered, these seven wondrous ones, in the house of Uri Ben-Zion, and Uncle Abie Cordo greeted them with honor, as befits young energetic lawyers, merchants, and contractors, most of them officers in the reserves with the appropriate ranks.

"Gentlemen," said Uncle Cordo, "it's important that you know what has happened. Whenever there's a war somewhere, immediately money follows and people get rich. They get rich all of a sudden, and they don't know what to do with the money. But, gentlemen, our ancient sages, of blessed memory, have said: Three things broaden a man's mind—a fine woman, a fine home, and fine accessories. Twenty years ago I was in Europe and I said to myself: Women, homes, accessories? All right, we'll take it in that order. To give them women I've missed the train. All the clubs in Germany and all the pleasure houses in Hamburg, already the Ashkenazis from the Land of Israel have put their hands on it. Apart from which, I'll tell you the truth: it's not pleasant to be in that business. There's plenty of profit, but hardly any honor. So what was left for me? Homes and accessories. So I said to myself: What does the newly rich person want? What his wife incites him to. Beautiful new clothes that cost millions. So I went and made a business of fashion. Now, gentlemen, you may ask why Mr. Cordo of Paris, London, and Munich comes to us to addle our brains about this. I'll give you the answer. Listen carefully. Only a month ago I took a holiday to return and come back to the land of my ancestors. I opened my eyes and walked in every town and everywhere I saw everyone sitting in a villa, or at least in a penthouse on a roof. I saw that the people are buying things for their homes, and in particular I saw that they're buying paintings with original signatures, and for them they pay fortunes. Now I tell you: Make business with pictures, the handmade originals. And how should you start? Start like me, from the home, not from the shop. Each of you in his own home can invite guests and bring along the original, the one who makes the pictures. And you serve drinks and talk sense. Believe me, there is millions in it. There will not be one single rich man who won't buy at least two pictures. And once he starts to buy, he won't stop. It's an investment, and it

is a luxury investment, because the picture doesn't ask
for food, and there is no tax on it, and there is no need
for storage. It hangs on the wall, and hangs until the
price goes up. This is the offer, gentlemen."

Uri's secretary served hot pastries called *burekas*, and
the assembled ones looked at each other and smiled. Not
because they had heard a joke, but because the speaker's
words had reached their hearts, because the speaker had
aimed so well at what they already knew a little bit from
their own experience.

And when the evening extended into the night, and
their hearts opened up by dint of the drinks, Ron,
Yaron, Laron *et al.* and also Shmuelsohn told things
which until then they had kept to themselves and had
not disclosed to one another. But now, after Abie Cordo
had opened the sluice, the facts poured into the room as
if a sewer had burst all at once.

And this was the gist of the story: This land of ours is
a land of ingratitude and requites the best of her sons
with evil for good. All of us here, Ron, Yaron, Laron
et al. and also Shmuelsohn, we have done something for
this country. Some of our best friends have paid with
their lives so that we could live here. Logic says that we
should be remunerated a little and be let to live in peace,
but no. Week after week, and especially on Fridays, the
telephone rings, from the Foreign Office, or the Information Office, or the Jewish Agency, and they have a
demand to make of us: to serve as host for the Sabbath
dinner in our house for some worthy Jew from America

or Belgium. Some Jew who once gave a contribution to the national funds, and has now come to the country with the old wife and the old spinster daughters, and he insists and demands to eat at the table of some important Israeli. So for this we are important? They torment us and don't let us spend a Sabbath in the bosom of our family. But what? We are people who have a sentiment of national responsibility, and we don't refuse. And thus on every Friday evening we sit at home with some *hittel-macher** from the Bronx or some diamond merchant from Antwerp, and we are dying of boredom. And we keep silent and we don't complain. But there is a limit to everything. And all of a sudden you get fed up and you say to your wife: If we get a call today from the Foreign Office, you can tell them that we have traveled to a foreign country. But the wife all of a sudden says no. And she has an interesting story to tell me: It's already happened twice and more that one of those Jews, who are full up to the throat with money, saw some painting on our wall and asked if it was authentic Israeli art. Between one thing and another he asked to buy it, and my wife didn't ask me, and sold to him. Of course she didn't lose on it. Tzippi, I say to her, you're a genius. And Tzippi says to me: More than you think. A month ago I went to an art gallery and I took six authentic pictures on consignment, and I sold them here in our house, under your nose, and you didn't even notice.

---

*Hatmaker.

After all, you never pay attention to me at all. And you don't care what I do. That's what Tzippi said to me. I saw that it is so, I told her: All right, we won't be in a foreign country this week, and we'll see how it goes. And what do you think? It went. Now we send a driver to the galleries with a car every week, and we load up the car with Israeli art on consignment, and on Sunday we pay the gallery and take more.

Ron, Yaron, Laron *et al.* and also Shmuelsohn said: You've taken the words out of our mouths. That's just exactly what's been going on in our homes too for half a year now.

Toward the end of the night the friends summed up to Abie Cordo and thus they said to him, "You see, you haven't told us anything new, and we owe you nothing. But we will say to you thank you very much. And more than that: from now on we'll call this entire operation by your name, Operation Cordo."

"Call it Operation Cordoviero," asked Abie, "because Cordoviero is a precious and honorable name in the history of our people, and for generations upon generations we have been dealing also with the Torah and the Kabbalah. And we also had documents to prove that we are from the family of King David. Except that those documents got burned up. Ask Uri."

25.

WHEN ABIE CORDO—in the speech he whispered into the ears of the friends—said that our people is essentially a people of culture, he did not know himself how right he was in his speech. At any rate he was right in all that concerns women.

At the beginning of the flourishing of the art business in the homes of Ron, Yaron, Laron *et al.* and also Shmuelsohn, their wives Tzippi, Shosh, Shulah, Silvi *et al.* were wasting money on dresses which they would buy in the boutiques of Abie Cordo, until they reached the level of real princesses: a dress that was bought at the beginning of the month was used as a rag to wipe the dust by the end of the month, if it had not been stolen by the maid. But this primeval stage of clothing culture did not last very long. Very soon Tzippi, Shosh, Shulah, and Silvi came to the conclusion that in fact they were not market hawkers, but channels for the proliferation of Israeli art in the world and for the advancement of original creation. And from the moment that this idea arose in their hearts, the idea took root and developed and flourished so well that those channels were filled with humility and reached the conclusion that they had to study the history of art, if they wanted to be able to convince the buyers and to raise the prices; whoever was concerned with raising cultural values had to learn the profession.

And with the demand there arose the supply. In the backyards of the main streets, and also in the municipal buildings of the suburbs of Tel Aviv, courses opened in ceramics, in poetry, and in the history of art, and the wives enrolled in these courses and also met there poets and painters. At the end of such a course, which took a fortnight or a month, they would travel abroad for post-graduate study, and they would see the most important museums with their own eyes. Some of them returned arrayed with diplomas in interior architecture and in due course became famous as preeminent decorators, and they were given the task of decorating the apartments of the pillars of the generation, as well as government of-fices and nightclubs, where high-class prostitutes per-haps did not know how to appreciate art, but foremost hairdressers, who had also done graduate study abroad, in institutes for wigs and hair dying, knew how to appre-ciate the effort.

That overwhelming wave of artistic revival made its mark on almost every home which had a budget for cul-ture. At that same time in the homes of the prominent there appeared table lamps, for example, made of horse-shoes that were bent by special craftsmen, according to instructions from Tzippi, Shosh, Shulah, or Silvi. There also appeared table lamps made out of copper pots, in which previously the primitive wives of the Arabs used to cook their meals. There were also table lamps made out of ostrich eggs and there were table lamps made out of scales from a grocery shop, and there were table lamps made out of toilet bowls and bidets. Each house had its personal taste, and each household bought in its own special boutique, which manufactured especially for its clients, so that by the end of three or four years all the flats looked alike, which is to say that all of them were decorated according to personal taste, refined and characteristic of their occupants.

And from table lamps it is only one step to furniture custom-made for the best homes. Instead of a chair, a camel saddle (we have brought the primordiality of the desert into civilization, and it is an interesting and daring confrontation); instead of a table, a grinding stone from the tents of the Sinai Bedouin (the instrument with which they used to make flour for bread will now carry on it refined foreign food); and so spread the habit of sitting on the floor when guests came, and taking off one's shoes, because the slogan was Relaxation, which was the mark of liberation from petty-bourgeois conventions. Very soon everybody became free from all conventions, and when you came to an uppermost flat, your eyes would encounter the turned-inward big toes of the ladies lost in Leisure, when the toenails were painted black, green, or aluminum—a feast for the eyes, and also daring.

Culture reached the walls also, and on the shelves one could see archaeological collections, whatever the husbands brought home from the occupied territories whenever they went to serve in the reserves. In all the best houses one could find special clay pots, archaeological, bearing the signature of a Minister in Israel; he who knew the Minister personally received such potsherds as a gift; and he who was not so fortunate paid the full price, in shops in New York, when he was on a graduate trip there. And thus the archaeological items of the Land of Israel returned to their mother's cradle, in keeping with "And thy children shall come again to their own border"—one of the distinguishing marks of the generation of revival.

These were the great days of our country, days when people did not have to fight at the front, because they had won a war, and could therefore devote their lives to spiritual matters, to the refined matters which only he who is blessed with prosperity could afford to devote himself to. Fortune willed it that in this same period they invented in the world the pill against pregnancy, and this too liberated women from worry and made the average man younger, and thus the achievements of science were mingled with some of the pinnacles of culture and became a single mixture, easy to swallow and easy to emit with astonishing quickness in order not to miss any opportunity.

And so that women might have more spare time to swallow and to emit a maximum of culture and other refinements of life, to Tzippi Yaron there occurred a marvelous idea. On one of her trips which she took abroad with her husband and her children, she was the guest of one of the Jews who had bought pictures from her on a Friday night. And since the hospitality did not cost money, the Yaron family stayed with that Jew in New York for about a month, and before they set out to return to the motherland, Tzippi said to her hosts, "What about our leaving one of our children with you for the next school year, so he can learn English?"

The New York Jews agreed, and Tzippi returned home and told her girlfriends how she had managed to put one over on those naïve and rich *hittelmachers*.

"In addition to that," said Tzippi, "it won't do me any harm to have a little rest from housework. Especially since I plan to take a special course in batik and in enameling."

Shosh, Shulah, and Silvi listened to that, and they admired Tzippi with great envy.

When Shosh Laron, Shulah Oren, and Silvi Ronnen, they, their husbands and children, traveled abroad, they accomplished still more. Shosh left three children with a Jewish millionaire in London for two years, Shulah left twins in Paris, and Silvi left her only son for temporary adoption in Los Angeles. This son was not especially bright, and he found it very difficult to take this separation from his parents, and when he wrote home that he was sick of his life because of the force of his homesickness, Silvi would read his letters to her friends and would interpret: "Look how he is attached to me. Show me another child who is so attached to his mother. Compare it with the youth in the Diaspora, those who smoke hashish and opium and run away from home. I have always said that the Israeli family is a paragon and an example of the marvelous tie between parents and their children."

When a car ran over Silvi's son and he was returned to his mother's home packed in plaster, Silvi took care of him with extreme devotion, until he became capable of walking on his feet with the aid of crutches. For a whole year she nursed him, and this was an additional proof of the depth of attachment and force of feeling within Israeli families.

Her girlfriends were bursting with envy and spent a lot of time hatching schemes to outdo her even in an achievement of this order.

And some of them succeeded in doing that.

It's really unbelievable. But it's a fact.

And whilst the women were liberating themselves and proliferating art, and were immersed in Leisure at home, in their boutiques, and in their backyards, it so happened that the fate of the male was not so fortunate. For this is the fate of males sometimes, in certain societies where man is supposed to be a hero. And who is a hero? The man whose wife is contented with him, because he does what is incumbent upon him.

As for our male, Leisure was far from him, inasmuch as the more money he had in hand the more he had to know where to invest it. There were men who became silent partners in butcher shops; and there were others, more refined, who felt queasy about butcher shops and bought steak houses. But since they had no expertise in such business they lost money, and very soon they started to go to attorneys and stockbrokers. And it is a notorious fact that he who holds securities peruses the stock-exchange columns of the newspapers. And so it was that in the early morning every male in Israel turned his eye to the stock-exchange columns and sure enough he found that some of his securities had risen in price and others had fallen. About the rises he was a bit glad, but about the falls he grieved greatly, and that day was already ruined for other matters. When he came to his office he would ring his stockbroker, and in the afternoon he would ring him again, to find out at what price he had sold.

Before all the good things of these years were bestowed upon us, the Israeli male used to read about politics in the papers, and took an interest in knowing whether the armies of the enemy had increased in strength, and whether there was a danger of war. If he read a hostile declaration from the mouth of one of the enemy leaders, he would remember that he would have to stand on guard; and when he went to serve in the reserves he would do his job faithfully. But now, when he read in the newspaper that the enemy had increased his force, he would say to himself: There's no cause for alarm. Just as we have defeated them up to now, so we will beat them in the future too. And he would immediately turn back to the stock-exchange columns, because the problems between us and the enemy would be solved by the army; but who would solve the problems of his investments in securities? Only God has the solutions. And on this point, on the godly point, these males were partners to that thin strand of repentance which was in vogue during those years: He who wrought miracles on the battlefield, could He not look favorably upon a matter of such little value as securities?

In such a situation there was no room, of course, for Relaxation, and not even for enjoying the culture which filled the home and life as the waters cover the sea.

A man goes with his wife to the theater like one impelled by the devil. He sits at the performance and trembles over what he will find tomorrow in the newspaper. Of course he does not pay attention to all the wisdom and beauty which the play seeks to bestow upon him. When he leaves the performance and goes to dine in a chic restaurant he is incapable of conducting a pleasant conversation about the theater and does not know whether he thought the play was good or bad, though in this matter it is possible to rely on the critics, who will write in the newspaper next morning and make it clear to the audience whether they had enjoyed themselves in the theater last night or whether they had been disappointed. But when there is no time to read reviews—from where will come pleasure?

And when there is no contentment in the heart, a man looks far away. And what does he see, far away? He sees a 'bank in Switzerland, and there he deposits some money. Come what may, Ron, Yaron, Laron *et al.* and also Shmuelsohn now started sending money to Switzerland, so that at least when they reach old age they would be able to rest from their toil. And so that their old age would not put their youth to shame, a lot of money would be needed in their old age. But from where is much money to be got, if the price of securities drops all of a sudden or some steak house goes broke?

And so it is possible to take something from the party coffer, or exert pressure on contractors and accept what are called bribes. It may not be acceptable, and also it may not be fair, for someone who just takes. But people who all their lives only gave and gave and gave to the nation, to the State and to the party, why should they not enjoy a little bit for themselves in their old age, in Switzerland?

In due course—after some time—they were caught, Ron, Yaron, Ronnen, Laron *et al.*, and they were sentenced to various periods of imprisonment, because the law is blind and does not take account of rights. Their colleagues understood all the same and reacted to the sentences with fury, and even helped Tzippi, Shosh, Shulah, and Silvi to get to the closed bank accounts in Switzerland. They had the know-how and there were contacts.

Only Shmuelsohn was not tried and was not sentenced to prison, because he agreed to serve as State's witness. At the last moment he faltered. But this step too was received among his colleagues with understanding and with gratitude too: he told only on those who had been caught.

Requiem for Na'aman

Uri Ben-Zion was somewhat distant from all these good things bestowed upon us: he did not buy pictures, he did not transfer money to Switzerland, he did not even buy securities. Deep down he was a scion of a family of farmers. And although he had not been born in the settlement in the south, where his family on his father's side had had its beginnings, the working of the land was nevertheless closer to his heart than the refined matters of culture. Therefore he bought tractors, bull-dozers, and steam shovels, with which he would make great excavations and build fortifications for the army. The amount of sand and clay, limesoil and loess which Uri moved with his machines from one place to another during those six years was inestimably greater than the amount of earth that his great-grandfather, Ephraim Abramson, had turned over in all the days of his long life.

But his uncle on his mother's side, Uncle Abie Cordo, had no understanding of this at all, and he asked Uri, "What actually do you make your livelihood from mainly?"

"From earthworks for the fortifications," said Uri with pride.

"What do you need earthworks for?" Abie Cordo flung at him impatiently. "First of all, there won't be any more wars because we've broken them forever. Sec-ondly, if there will be a war what use are fortifications? After all, what can the sand, and even the concrete, do against the modern catapults and the secret death-rays?"

"Uncle Abraham," said Uri, "you deal with your

women's underwear. That's something you understand much better."

"Really?" Abie Cordo mocked him. "And you think your fortifications are stronger than underpants? Look here, if somebody wants to rape a lady, the underpants fall down easily."

"If you're such an expert on women, why aren't you married?" answered Uri, beside the point, because he was angry, and because he was not so sure that his uncle was mistaken.

"I've tried that already and I canceled the marriage. If I want a woman, I make a telephone call," said Abie Cordo. "And also when your fortifications go up into the air, you'll make a telephone call. America you'll telephone and you'll ask for help. Ha, what do you say to that?"

"It's a pity that you came here," said Uri. "You could have stayed quietly where you were."

"It's a pity that you did not spend a few years where I was," said Cordo. "Perhaps you would have accumulated a bit of *proporzione*, so that you could see better."

And thus ended their conversation, for the time being.

26.

UNTIL THE YEAR 1973 arrived. Or to be more precise: the sixth of October 1973. For on the fifth of October quite a number of paintings were still sold to quite a number of tourists from Brazil and Colombia. But in the morning on the sixth of October warning sirens were heard and people were called up to their units and they did not know precisely why or wherefore.

Some of the officers in the reserves and not in the reserves were torn away from their investments by the cruel hand of fate, and all of a sudden they remembered that they had not given orders for the lubrication of the engines in the tanks under their command since they had lost part of their investments in the steak houses and in the cosmetics industry. Others were really alarmed when they realized that for more than three months they had not checked the condition of the ammunition in the stores which were under their command. Needless to say, they immediately—that very moment—neglected all their business affairs and rushed to their units. The same rule applied to Ministers and heads of committees and directors of departments. Every one of them ferreted through his files and found the minutes from which he was destined to prove that he had warned about what was about to happen, but no one had listened to him. And what was about to happen—is it not that we shall know soon enough, if not today then tomorrow? It is not possible to hide the needle in the haystack, and also in the end the awl will peep out of the sack. Or perhaps this whole thing was a hoax. Another election maneuver initiated by the ruling party? Or perhaps this time the Opposition was to blame?

Benjamin Tammuz

The first victims fell at the Suez Canal and on the Golan Heights; the lines of fortification that Uri had built collapsed. One of the Ministers was already holding the microphone in his hand in order to announce to the nation that everything was lost; but one woman journalist burst out crying, and another journalist alerted the Prime Minister, and thus the public was deprived of an unauthorized announcement.

Only after a few days did the unlubricated machinery recover, and whilst the soldiers in the front line were paying with their lives the price of the securities and the table lamps, the army launched its counteroffensive, and again the miracle happened. But this time the number of victims was four times greater than it had been in 1967. The military victory was decisive and terrible, as it had been in every one of the previous wars, but it missed the deadline.

"If you support the Jews," said the enemy to the nations of the world, "you will not get oil."

And the world replied: "We are not alarmed by the threat, and we shall always act according to our moral principles, but we have never supported the unjustified demands of the Jews, and today too we are prepared to vote against them in every case where Israel endangers the peace of the world or violates the laws."

And Israel—as in days gone by—endangers the peace of the world and violates the laws; and justly she was hastily thrown out of Unesco which is the United Nations organization of culture and science, in order to make room for the luminaries of science and art which are so numerous in the Middle East.

No one in Israel understood what had happened, because had they understood, they would not have been able to stand it. The number of dead and wounded and of those afflicted in their hearts was greater than the people's ability to mourn. If they had looked in the mirror they might have found the guilty one, and therefore they broke all the mirrors in the State, and he who walked in the street saw only the other's face. Then people locked themselves in their houses, out of sheer disgust. And if they longed to meet a friend with whom one could open one's heart, it transpired that this friend had been killed in the war.

"Where is that God who was revealed to you in 1967, in the moment of danger?" someone asked his friend the officer who had discovered Divine Providence at that time.

But the one who was asked could not answer, because he had been killed in the war.

And also the one who had asked did not continue to ask, because he was one of the war dead.

Only the politicians went on talking, until the people spat in their faces and raised others in their place. And immediately the new ones began talking.

Abie Cordo, just as he had waited about half a year after the victory of 1967 and only then returned to the land of his forefathers, just so he waited about half a year after the defeat of 1973, and only then left the land of his forefathers and returned to the Diaspora. And why did he decide to leave us? The floor to Abie Cordo:

"You listen to me, Uri, one thing is very important. The basis of life is harmony. Day and night. Light and dark. Rich and poor. Men and women. That's the simple secret. And if the harmony is broken, life is completely tasteless. Now, let's look at what has happened to you in the Land of Israel. Suddenly the harmony was broken, at the moment that three thousand five hundred young men were killed. True, it is really a great disaster for the members of their families, and this itself is really terrible, but if it happens to a nation like the Chinese, or even the French, what then? They have millions of people and according to statistics it's as if nothing has happened to them at all. But among you it's different. The moment the three thousand five hundred young people are missing, immediately you get a surplus of women over men. The woman no longer has the same chance of getting married as she had before. And you should know that the best client for the fashion business is the young woman, the one who has married not long ago, or the woman whose husband is making good profits. Now, where will the weddings come from? And who will be making good profits in the near future? So, if I look at my business, I can see that it's finished in this country for quite a few years to come, and I have to pack up the suitcases and go. But this is not at all the main thing. The main thing is what I told you previously about harmony. The surplus of women over men has one specific bad symptom: the male no longer needs to court the girl.

The male is very much wanted, and becomes arrogant and audacious. There is no more *chevalerie*, no manners. He goes straight to the point, pulls down the underpants and pushes her onto the bed. And I can't live in a place like that. There's a minimum of *finesse* in life that I won't forgo. And therefore out of sorrow, and believe me, also with a broken heart, I'm walking out."

"Uncle Abraham," said Uri, who had listened in silence to this very instructive lesson, "tell me, do you know of a good bank in Switzerland where I can deposit a sum of money quietly and in confidence?"

Uncle Abraham promised to arrange this matter efficiently and safely, and asked Uri if perhaps he wanted to invest a little bit in the fashion houses in London, Paris, and Munich.

To this Uri replied that he would think about it. He had not yet decided.

27.

Sixty years of age was Oved when that war broke out, and he was prevented from participating in it bodily. During the whole month of October he employed all his contacts, telephoning to staff officers and to corps commanders, and received angry replies from their secretaries and adjutants, until one day someone put his mind at rest and told him that Uri had been seen in the south, and that he was well. Later on Uri himself rang his

parents and told them that he had recuperated from a
slight injury and had returned to his unit. Rachel and
Oved started roaming in their car from one military hospital to another, because they thought that Uri was still
lying wounded in one of them, until it turned out that
he had not lied to them, because he arrived in Jerusalem
for one night, standing on his own legs, lean and suntanned. Rachel burst out crying and Oved stroked the
face of his son, like a blind man trying to prove with his
own fingers that he is not being made a fool of. That
night Uri slept fourteen hours, and his parents turned
restlessly on their bed and Oved scolded Rachel and
said, "Why don't you sleep, Rachel? Our house is now
full of goodness."

"Now, yes," said Rachel. "But what kind of month
have we had?"

"We've passed it," said Oved, "and we have to forget.
Think about what has happened in other houses. Look
how God has had mercy on us."

"Why all of a sudden did you say God? In my family,
four souls were lost."

"I don't know. It just came out of my mouth," apologized Oved; he turned on the light of the lamp and lit
himself a cigarette. "Shall we make coffee, huh?"

Coffee, *kebab*, *shishlik*, kubbeh* and pickles, whiskey
and French cognac, *hoummous* and *pittas* warmed over

---

*A cigar-shaped rice cake filled with mutton and deep fried.

charcoal, steaks of mutton and bottles of wine were all laid out in the summerhouse, in the sitting room, in the yard, in the restored ruin, and on the lawn, awaiting the guests who had been invited to the gathering, in the spring of 1974.

This gathering might have been arranged even earlier, but somehow Oved knew in his heart that it should wait. Firstly, those of his friends who had lost a son or a brother might not come at all. And those who had emerged from the war more or less unscathed might not feel inclined for gatherings in such days. Many of his officer friends had been explicitly mentioned in the newspapers, by name and rank, and they received cold shoulders and criticism bitter as gall, whilst those who were fortunate and had been overlooked might perhaps be afraid to come, lest they be told to their faces that it was only by chance that the headlines had not jumped on them.

It was also clear to Oved that the gathering would not be joyful, like the one that was held in honor of Grand-father Ephraim's jubilee; nor did he have the intention, this time, of urging the participants to tell tales of war and heroism. Only this did he desire in his heart: not to disrupt the tradition, so as not to sever the thin, fragile, and precarious thread which made possible the pretense that it was still in its power to link the people to the good old days.

And lo and behold, they did come. Also some of those who had been wounded. They came in their cars, came into the house somewhat stooped, as if the doors were too low and the ceiling were pressing slightly upon the skull. One rubbed his hands together as if there were a frost in the air. Or perhaps this was the movement of approaching the job, the job of eating and drinking, seeing the abundance on the tables? Army men have strong nerves and they have a sense of humor of their own. One can never know. One came in and looked around, as if he were searching for someone in particular —someone who could join him against a possible attack, or perhaps someone who was already not among the living, but in spite of it had bothered to come here, out of habit? And when they greeted each other, they spoke in whispers, as if they were afraid to awaken sleepers.

Herzl too was among those who came. But it was no longer the Herzl of days gone by. His straight carriage had not bent, but it seemed as if it had been broken in the middle. He still walked erect, but anyone who saw him sensed that at his navel he was broken. And any breeze might topple him onto the floor: so light was he, like a splinter hovering and being carried to another place.

Bella-Yaffa, aged thirty-eight, who a few years back had needed special treatment, had come back to the summerhouse and returned to her occupations and she was also assisting Yonas-Yehoshuah Bieberkraut, aged fifty-seven, in the compilation of his dictionary. In those days they were on the letter *B*. They both came down from their rooms on the upper floor and came and sat near Herzl, watching the gathered.

Requiem for Na'aman

For none of those gathered was this the first visit to the summerhouse, yet they all behaved as if they had come to a strange place, which had to be sounded out before deciding in which corner one might land and to whom one might clutch. Or perhaps they had been invited in order to be insulted? They roamed around the sitting room, came out into the yard, peered into the restored ruin, and scarcely stretched out their hands to the dishes. To himself each one passed in his mind's eye over the previous gatherings in this place, and he knew that what had been would not be again, not here and not in the place to which they would return when the gathering was over.

Actually they knew that they were people under whose feet the ground had dropped away. The glitter of rank was dimmed, and the charm of the eternally victorious had vanished, and even the terrible victory, costly and dreadful, that they had bought on the battlefield would not restore the honor they had had before. Who was the betrayer? Who was the betrayed? How had such a thing happened? About half a year had passed since the end of the war, and still the questions were hanging in the air and the people too seemed to be hovering in a kind of hazy space. This gathering that Oved Ben-Zion had arranged to commemorate the twenty-sixth Independence Day of the State was like being summoned by command, and the people obeyed the command; but they were still expecting an explanation to come from the mouth of the summoner. Here, we've come, and now tell us what mean ye by this service?

Here and there little groups began to assemble and soon came apart and dispersed. Those who flocked together turned an ear, and found that no one gave an explanation. So they returned to wandering around the house and the yard. Someone remembered that years ago Yonas-Yehoshuah Bieberkraut had made a speech here, a sort of funny speech, emotional, confused; perhaps he had something to say this time too? If there is no one better, even a madman would do, provided that the empty unbearable void would be filled.

So somebody walked up to the place where Herzl and Bella-Yaffa and Bieberkraut were sitting, and said, "Hello, sir, how are you? It's been a long time since we saw you or heard you."

But Bella-Yaffa guessed that they were trying to make fun of Bieberkraut, and she also guessed that they were not doing this out of malice, but out of an emptied and an angry heart. So she pointed to a nearby chair and said, "Sit down here, please, we might talk a bit. . . . And perhaps also the others would like to come over. . . . I'd like to say a few words."

Although what she said was said calmly and in a whisper, the message passed like fire through a field of dry thorns which was stricken by drought: thus the drowning man is endowed with supreme sensitivity when a straw is thrown to him into the deep waters. At first those approached who were near where Bella-Yaffa was sitting, and afterward they beckoned to those further off, and soon the yard was emptied and the room was filled.

Requiem for Na'aman

"Friends and acquaintances," said Bella-Yaffa, "forgive me for being so daring. . . . I listened for many years to your stories. . . . My father told me that I should listen to you carefully, so that I could learn from you and take example. . . . And verily I did listen, and also my brother, Uri, he listened to you, and he also became like one of you. . . . Sometimes I do not sleep at night, and I think of you. . . . Don't think that I don't see. Surely you will understand. . . . You are not guilty. . . . You are not guilty. And you know why you are not guilty? Because you are floating and sailing within the dream of other people, who have died long ago. They, the others, have dreamed a dream, many years ago, and you are the materialization of that dream. All in all you have fulfilled what you were commanded to do in the dream of those other people. . . . And they too, the first dreamers, are not guilty. They could not have known how those dreams of theirs would descend into reality and take shape in it. . . . How could they have known a thing like that? Here something else has happened. . . . And perhaps there is someone who deludes all of us? How is it possible otherwise to understand all this? And after all we wanted all this to be so very different, we wanted other things. . . . All of us seek some elusive truth, and we are pursuing it. . . . And surely it is impossible for us not to obtain it one day, or at least see it from afar, like Moses, who saw the Land. . . . In spite of all, he did see, with his own eyes. . . . And that's a lot, that's almost all that one can expect. . . . And perhaps I am a foolish woman, speaking about herself, saying idle talk. . . . And you will bear with me."

And whilst the silence still held within it the last stammerings of her thin and hollow voice, Yonas-Yehoshuah Bieberkraut leapt up from his chair and shouted into the empty space of the room, "Just one word, one single sentence, and immediately I'll return to my silence. Well, it's like this. . . . Of the absolute we have no idea whatsoever on account of our essential limitations. . . . And so, he who tries to grasp the absolute, he is wrestling with the angel. Look out, I have warned you."

He immediately sat down in his chair and buried his face with his hands.

"What? What was that?" several voices were heard around.

The people, who had not understood, were nevertheless angry with the things they had just heard.

"It seems to me that I have understood," Uri volunteered to explain. "If I'm not mistaken about what Doctor Bieberkraut has said, then he wanted to say something like this, more or less: If people take too seriously the ideas which they themselves contemplate . . . if someone has some idea, and he starts believing that it wasn't born in his own belly, but on Mount Sinai, for example, or it just came to him directly from Divine Providence . . . in that case everything is finished. This is the end. The trouble with every ideology is that when you say you're prepared to die for it, you mean in practice that you're prepared to kill for it. Every ideology is a license for murder, just as it is an offer for suicide. So first of all one has to rise against the idealist inside him, and kill him. That will be the last murder that a human being would commit. . . . And why do I say all these things right now, after 1973? Because the shit we are immersed in, all of us, is a direct result . . . because we have done evil in the eyes of the Lord. . . . I'm not trying to tell you that I've discovered God. I'm repeating a verse from the Bible because it's an apt verse, and it hits the target. We've done disgraceful things, gentlemen, all of us. . . . And what did we actually do? We built fortifications and we made several good thousands. And what did others do? They sold paintings to *hittelmachers* from New York. And others simply robbed the chest, without giving anything in return. They didn't even bother to spread a bluff, for the sake of good order. . . . I don't come here to confess and to repent; I'm also not preaching. It's too late. I have come to say that if you serve a great ideology, then you allow yourself an awful lot. . . . As you're even prepared to die for it, then in the meantime is it forbidden to commit a few nasty things? That's why I say: Let us lower our ideals, let us give them a human scale. . . . That's quite low, but it can be done. The other thing cannot be done."

"Uri,"—the voice of one of the generals was heard. It was clear that he had waited patiently for the speech to end, and immediately after it ended he started and said, "Listen, Uri, I knew you were a lawyer, but I didn't know you were also a psychologist, a philosopher, and a prophet. I won't get into a dispute with you here, but I'll make only one comment. When people set before themselves a high and exalted ideal, then there is a little chance, though almost none, that they will achieve some small percentage of the ideal. There is also a chance that if not all of them would be ready to die for it, at least they would be ready to make some small contribution, though sometimes no more than an annual membership fee. But if they will seriously accept your suggestion and they will lower the ideal to what you call a human scale, the same thing will happen: they will realize only a negligible percentage of that ideal. In other words, according to your suggestion, almost nothing."

"Please," said Uri, "here are two proposals and we can put them to the vote. Is there anyone here who feels himself to be so pure that he will dare to raise his hand?"

"Uri, don't exaggerate," answered the general. "I, for example, did not sell paintings and I did not profit from fortifications. But even he who did so is still entitled to vote, if it's a question of voting. You know why all of us are entitled to vote? Because some of us did die. And that includes people who are now here with us in this house. You understand me, Uri? Or should I go on and explain?"

"Enough," said Uri. "I admit that we have gone a bit too far. Enough for today. For me, anyway."

"For me, too," the general agreed with him.

The people who had been standing around on their

feet all this time now started dispersing and at long last approached the tables. Very quickly the *kebab* and the *shishlik* and the steaks and the pickles and the *pittas* with the *hoummous* started to disappear. Then the bottles began to be emptied, and in the late hours of the night, when the guests started dispersing to return to their homes, one who looked from the side might have believed that here was the place where a good Independence Day party had taken place, as in those good old days.

And the general did not forget to report to Bella-Yaffa to obtain a special farewell blessing from her.

"In contrast to what your brother said," he told her, "I accept the things you said and I will think about them a lot."

The general kissed Bella-Yaffa's hand and even waved goodbye to her from the threshold; and she thought to herself that if the world were different and the time were another time and she another woman, then the general could have been the man about whom a woman like herself might have entertained certain thoughts. What thoughts she did not know exactly. She did not have the experience, and the hour was late.

Herzl remained the night in the summerhouse, and when Uri accompanied him to his room on the upper floor, his grandfather's brother turned to him and said: "I'm remaining here, Uri. I've come to die among the family. Tell this to your mother and see to it that they'll care for me a bit. It won't last very long."

211

28.

Joy was far from the hearts of Bella-Yaffa and Doctor
Bieberkraut, because the work on the dictionary did not
turn out well, and from year to year added difficulties
were heaped up on their path. It became clear that instead of items arranged and interpreted, instead of nouns
at the side of which would appear a clear explanation,
the dictionary was destined to be paved with question
marks, shruggings of shoulders, and unsolved problems.

Seemingly, from the purely scientific point of view,
there would be no difficulty in this, since in fact posing
the question is the decisive step in any serious scientific
approach. All this is so, seemingly, and generally, but
not in the case before us.

Yonas-Yehoshuah Bieberkraut had not set his heart on
just making a dictionary, but wanted to build a bridge
across the abysses of time, and to give into the hands of
the student that redeeming and delivering Ariadne's
thread which, if you hold it by its end, empowers you to
bridge the road that lies between the time in which you
stand today and the time when the people of Israel were
exiled from its land, some two thousand years ago.

If Bieberkraut's idea is hard to understand in its ab-
stract form, one could give a concrete example. You're
walking along on the stony ground of the slopes of the

hill sloping down into Wadi Millk and your foot stumbles on a small stone. You lift up the stone and examine it. If you are aware of geology you know immediately that the stone is *Basalt* or *Schiefer** or *Granit* or *Quartz*. But in our particular case, geological awareness is not at all sufficient, because you do not know the Hebrew name of this stone. The names of the stones in the Bible include riddles and puzzles, like *shoham*, *pitda*, *ekdah*, *yahalom*, *leshem*, *halamish*, *tzur*, and other linguistic Fata Morgana.

And now, we shall commence with the letter *aleph**: the word *ekdah*. Nowadays we call a pistol *ekdah* in Hebrew. Why? Bieberkraut holds that this is a complete distortion. A pistol is something to shoot with and *ekdah* is a stone from among the stones in the breastplate of the High Priest. And how will we ever know the true nature of that stone named *ekdah?*

You might say: What's the calamity if we don't know?

To that Bieberkraut would say: The calamity is total. If it is not possible to reach across time with a linguistic bridge, how will we build an emotional bridge, or an ideological one? Is it not language that ministers to reason and emotion at once? Hence, if the work on this dictionary does not turn out well, what is there for the Jews to do in the Land of Israel? They will go to America, or to England, or to France, or to Germany, and

---

* Slate.

* The Hebrew letter A or E.

there all the nouns will be lucid to them. It is impossible for human beings to live whole intellectual lives unless they have a clear knowledge, a complete hold upon the corporeal reality of the world.

In the year 1974 the two of them reached the letter *B;* not because the letter *A* had come out whole and intact under their hands, but because they had compiled and refined everything that there is to the letter *A*, but in most cases they cleared out their matter with question marks, like this: ?, or like this: (?), or like this: [?], everything according to the necessity of the matter, and according to the system that Bieberkraut had established.

On winter days they worked in the large room on the ground floor, and on summer days they laid out their papers on tables in the restored ruin. And so as to stop the pages from flying in the wind they would place on them stones from the stones of the place, without knowing the names of these stones.

They would sit together in the restored ruin and their hearts swarmed with doubts. Bieberkraut would lift his weary eyes from the paper before him, and then he would see the two trees that had been planted there, on either side of the Roman sarcophagus.

"What kind and what name is this tree in our language?" He hurls a challenging question toward Bella-Yaffa.

She looks at the trees and says, *"Brosh."*

She knows she has made a mistake, but she is speaking in a Hebrew idiom of the people, because this is one of

214

the tasks Bieberkraut has given her within the framework of their work.

"*Brosh?*" Bieberkraut blurts out angrily. "And this, where do you get that from? What we do know is that the name of this tree is *cypress* in English, for example. But how do you know that this is *brosh?* And now, let us see what they have pointed out to us, our dictionary sages."

And with the dexterity of a sorcerer his fingers grasp Alcalay's dictionary (Hebrew-English) and he reads from it: "*Brosh (broshim, broshei-)*—cypress, pine."

"And now," he shouts in a triumphant blast, "already now it is clear to us on the authority of Alcalay that a *brosh* is perhaps a cypress or perhaps a pine. Now let's turn to another scholar. For example, what will we learn from that great light, the Megiddo dictionary (English-Hebrew), on the meaning of the English word *cypress?*"

Again his fingers dart among the pages and find, "Cypress—*teashur* (needle tree)."

"You see?" he sprays sparks. "Now the cypress is the *teashur*. Which means that the *brosh* and the *teashur* are one and the same, according to Alcalay and Megiddo. But the comedy has not ended. Now let's see what Alcalay says about the *teashur*."

And immediately the disrepute of these dictionaries is revealed publicly. In Alcalay it is written simply, "*Teashur (teashurim, rei-)*—teashur."

"Aha," roars Bieberkraut. "You see how far his wisdom goes? But this time he's honest, and tells us simply:

I don't know. And now, which is the tree that we are to call *brosh*? Is it the cypress or the pine or, perhaps, heaven forbid, *teashur*? And you, Bella-Yaffa, made haste to tell us that this tree in front of us is nothing but a *brosh*. Just so, without checking. '*Brosh*, *tidhar* and *teashur* together,' as it is written in the Bible. Is it possible that the author of the book meant in truth to write '*Brosh*, *brosh* and *brosh* together?' And we still haven't checked the views of the scholars on *tidhar*. I can imagine in my mind what they've come up with in their great wisdom. Here, see how lies rule over all, inescapably!"

Bella-Yaffa hastily leafed in Alcalay's dictionary and found "*tidhar*—elm tree (?)" and showed it to Bieberkraut.

"Well, here in front of us is a more successful case," said Bieberkraut. "At least the author admits his ignorance and writes a question mark. *Nu*, now back to our work."

Not every day did they sit at work on the dictionary. Sometimes Bieberkraut was struck by wanderlust and would pick up a rucksack and would walk among the hills for a whole day. Then Bella-Yaffa would be attacked by dread and worried that if what had happened to her several years ago happened to her again, there would be no one to summon help. When she was immersed with Bieberkraut in working on the dictionary she was given over to a framework of discipline, bent to the emphatic laws of reason that emanated forcefully from Yonas-Yehoshuah's personality. Yet it was not only reason which radiated from his personality, but also some other force, very tiring, demanding, annoying, and a bit beyond Bella-Yaffa's ability to endure; but without his very presence she would have collapsed long ago. This is what she had believed of late; and in the evening hours, if he was late in returning, she knew that if he did not return at once the end would come. But Bieberkraut always returned, and on his return he seemed to be filled with new energy and new forces without which who knows whether he would have been able to continue with his life's work.

After such a day of anxiety and expectation about his return Bella-Yaffa would retire to her room appeased, but very tired, and she was unable to sleep. Half-awake, with her eyes closed, she would be attended by kinds of dreams, which as a matter of fact were not dreams, because she was awake. They were kinds of elusive visions, something like a dream-preface; but the moment she turned her mind to these night visions they would vanish and disappear into wakefulness. She tried, therefore, by all kinds of cunning inventions, to hold onto the hems of those sights and to understand what they were showing her, because the matters in those visions were very important to her, although she did not understand their nature.

In those dream-prefaces she would see herself sometimes going out at night to the road at the skirts of the hills; and immediately across from there, on the other side of the road, another land would stretch itself, where people were expecting her to come. And when this vision disappeared and vanished, she wanted to remember who these people were, and she did not know; only this did she remember, that in the hands of every one of them there was a lighted candle. And when this vision returned, and Bella-Yaffa crossed the road and stood among them, they did not notice her, perhaps because she did not have a lighted candle in her hand.

One night she found herself walking among them and looking for familiar faces, although the faces of all those people had been known to her long ago. And then she heard one of them say to another:

"This is Bella-Yaffa who knows almost all the questions, but not one single answer."

And all of the audience seemed to hasten to run away and vanish and she remained alone and she emitted a cry of fear, and she went on wailing and begging them to come back and explain to her what the man had intended by his words.

One night Bella-Yaffa saw Ephraim Abramson galloping on a horse among the hills, and beckoning to her to join him. Soon the rider caught up with another galloping horse, on which a woman was riding. When he approached the woman he saw that it was Bella-Yaffa. The dreaming Bella-Yaffa looked at the Bella-Yaffa who was on the horse and saw that indeed it was she. Ephraim Abramson reached out his hand and felt the face of Bella-Yaffa on the horse, and Bella-Yaffa the dreamer said to him, "How do you know that Bella-Yaffa is Bella-Yaffa? Perhaps here a question mark is needed?"

"Nice work!" cried Bieberkraut's voice. "Pick up a stone from the stones of the place and throw it at Grandfather Ephraim."

Bella-Yaffa took a stone and threw it, and she knew that she had crushed Bieberkraut's skull, and she also knew that she had wanted to do so already long ago.

In the morning she told Bieberkraut her dream, and he listened to her without saying a word, but shortly afterward he went to the entrance of the house, and began to dial the telephone.

"What are you doing?" asked Bella-Yaffa, who had followed him on tiptoe.

"Perhaps it would be a good thing if I let Uri know. . . . It may be that you are in need of a physician," said Bieberkraut, when he was caught in the act.

"Put down the receiver," said Bella-Yaffa. "This is not a matter for physicians, this is something between you and me. And are not both of us here? So why do we need any mediators? Come, let us go and return to the work that is before us."

Bieberkraut obeyed, but when he turned toward the restored ruin, Bella-Yaffa did not walk with him, but she followed him with her eyes, and she did not move from her place in front of the house.

At noontime Yonas-Yehoshuah Bieberkraut disappeared and Bella-Yaffa went up to the room of the dying Herzl and told him that Bieberkraut had gone for a walk in the hills and would return in the evening. Herzl waved his hand and closed his eyes. He was tired and drowsed most of the hours of the day. Bella-Yaffa straightened the blanket under his feet and left the room in silence.

In the kitchen the old Arab woman was peeling vegetables and in the yard the old Arab was hoeing weeds from among the flowers. Bella-Yaffa went and stood near him, observing him in his work. The old Arab straightened up from his hoe, smiled and said, "The work, there's never an end to it. Only man is gradually being finished. Here, I hoe the weeds every year and I think to myself: At long last I've finished and I've got rid of them. But they just strike root in the earth and wait. I turn here and there, summer goes by, and here they are again, the accursed ones. They are laughing at us. Did I not speak the truth, Miss Bella?"

"And the names of these weeds, what are they, would you know?" asked Bella-Yaffa.

"*Injil*, they are called in our language," said the old man.

"Are you sure of that?" Bella-Yaffa continued to interrogate.

"Sure of what?" The old man did not understand the question.

"Are you sure that in Arabic the name of this weed is *injil?*"

"What do I care what its name is?" laughed the old man, "this weed has been breaking my back for fifty

220

years, and even if it had no name, cursed be it. From the sons of Satan it is, and not of God, of this I am sure."

Bella-Yaffa turned away from him and walked to the restored ruin. Heaps of papers were profuse there on two tables and on each pile there lay a stone. Bella-Yaffa picked up the stones carefully and arranged them in a straight column, one behind the other, on the floor of the ruin. Then she bundled all the papers into a single bundle and placed it inside an iron barrel, into which led a drainpipe to receive rainwater. Now the barrel was arid and empty. Then she went up to Yonas-Yehosh-uah's room and began to drag from there and to put into the barrel the dictionaries, the reference books and the bundles of manuscript on the letter *A*. At last she called to the old Arab and ordered him to set fire to all the papers.

The old man looked at the barrel filled above its brim and said, "The way they are here, they will not catch fire, because the fire needs air to breathe. If you agree, I'll take this rubbish to the place where we burn the dry *injil*, beside the fence."

"Good," said Bella-Yaffa. "I'm relying on you. And get to work immediately."

"As you say, Miss," said the old man, and went to bring the wheelbarrow.

After a short while an orange flame arose at the corner of the yard and thin pillars of smoke were carried up-ward into the peaceful summer air and climbed aloft. The smell of burning came to Herzl's nose and he groaned and went to the window and watched the bon-fire.

Bella-Yaffa saw him from her place in the restored ruin and she waved a greeting to him with her hand and Herzl replied to her with a wave of his hand and returned to his bed.

Late in the afternoon Bella-Yaffa went into the kitchen and took a candle and matches and placed them in the pocket of her dress. She did not have the patience to wait for dark to descend, and she set out toward the road, she crossed it and started walking toward the wadi, toward the place from which the people bearing the candles had come. If she did not find them there, she said to herself, she would come back at night to the fringes of the road, to the place where they gather and stand in any case.

Toward evening a Yemenite farmer, from the cooperative settlement opposite, was riding his ass on his way home, and Bella-Yaffa stood upright in his way, waved her arms and ordered him to stop.

"Listen," she said to him, "they murdered Bieber-kraut's brother with knives and they struck off his sexual member and they placed it inside his mouth."

"Who?" The Yemenite was alarmed. "Whom? Where was it?"

"The Arabs," said Bella-Yaffa. "Because he didn't know any of the names."

The Yemenite farmer said, "Where do you live, Miss? Where is your home? If you wish I will put you on my donkey and we will go to your home."

"I am going to my home," said Bella-Yaffa, "and Na'aman is expecting me there, and I have no need of a donkey. I am riding on a horse."

"On a horse?" said the Yemenite, and suddenly he remembered that in his home a lot of work was waiting for him, and the strange woman was well dressed, and surely she had relatives who would come at once and return her to her place. Therefore he kicked his ass and rode on his way.

Toward evening she stood on top of the hill, from where she could see the summerhouse. She bent down to the earth and started to collect weeds and dry grass and piled them into a pile. And when the pile was high enough, she took a match and set fire to the weeds. If they want to find me, she said to herself, they will know where to look for me. When the bonfire kindled and its flames burst out crackling upward, Bella-Yaffa turned and descended by the other side of the hill and sailed into the vineyards. When darkness descended Uri arrived in his car, and with him Yonas-Yehoshuah Bieberkraut. Uri turned immediately toward the house and Bieberkraut went into the restored ruin, and from there into his room. And when he saw that the papers and the books had disappeared he burst out shouting. The Arab couple told Uri what they had to tell, and Herzl said that he had seen a bonfire on top of the hill opposite, and he suggested that they go there first. Uri reached the hill escorted by the old Arab, and indeed they did find hot cinders and ashes from a bonfire of thorns that had gone out not long before, but they did not find Bella-Yaffa, and immediately they went back to the house and summoned the police by telephone.

Bella-Yaffa did not meet the candle-bearing people on her way, but she did see Ephraim Abramson several times from afar, galloping on his horse on the tops of the hills, following in the footsteps of those fleeing. Then she saw a pack of dead military men standing upright among the vines, and being sorry, and she told them that they should not be sad, because Bieberkraut would soon go back to his work, and this time the dictionary would turn out, and all the riddles would be deciphered, and there would be no room to say that the sacrifices had been for nought. But within her heart she wondered if indeed she was speaking the truth. In any case there was no doubt that in Hebrew *injil* is called *yablit*, and if Bieberkraut would be stubborn about this too, it would be possible to throw a stone at him, even if the name of the stone is not as clear as it should be. As the old Arab had said, "What do I care what its name is? The main thing is that it breaks my back."

A lone man came toward her on the road, he took her hand and kissed the back of her hand. Bella-Yaffa drew herself erect and said to him, "Now go on your way, and thou shalt not come back until thou findest Na'aman. And when thou seest him tell him only this: Bella-Yaffa is ready."

The man made a bow to her and went on his way.

Bella-Yaffa watched him a long while, and afterward,

when he had almost disappeared from sight, she waved her hand to him, whether in farewell or whether to signal him to come back, she did not know. And then she said, "Beloved."

And she listened to this new word in amazement. She was troubled by her daring and by the sweetness. "Beloved," she pronounced again, and the word was correct and beautiful. "And I, how is it I knew not?"

"Beloved," her thin voice dived and was washed upon the dry stones. "See now I have found you, and you are skipping upon the hills—to where are you slipping away?—and I am here, saying to you, Come, saying to you, Love, saying to you, vowing to you I was asleep and listening, my father and grandfather, all my uncles and brothers were building themselves houses, and we have no house, I had poem-words, you had troops, my songs sang you, your soldiers kept watch over our estate, the roads were parted and separated, my coat to my skin and to your flesh a uniform, barren until now, but no more, my man, I am yours and to you I go, no more alone, put your head on my shoulder, sleep a lover's rest, come back from the field of bloodshed I am with you, a spouse reserved from the beginning of time, inscribed to you, hovering to you, halt, halt from fleeing, I have no more strength in me to hover, hold my feet, hold them firmly, the angels are calling to me, do not let me be their booty, tear up the verdict whilst my feet are on earth, my lord, friend of my heart, strong and redeeming, merciful, don't loosen, see, see, see, look at me. Na'aman will say yes, he is brother to me."

The lone man looked at her from afar, his face covered with sadness, and its color was gray. The wind carried him and he crumbled like chaff.

Bella-Yaffa dropped onto the earth and the darkness covered her and pleaded with her to yield. She tried with all her strength not to be tempted, but her strength did not stand by her.

When she opened her eyes she found in the field two large stones, lying one facing the other. She sat down on them, Bella-Yaffa facing Bella-Yaffa, and she said, "Do you think that the candle-bearers will pass here?"

Said Bella-Yaffa, "I believe that they are already looking for us and perhaps it would be better if we get up and walk to the road."

"I am a little bit tired," said Bella-Yaffa, "and I would not like to be seen tired. I would like to unite with my dear ones when I am fresh and gay."

"Do you think they would let me remain with them?" said Bella-Yaffa.

"They will embrace you and they will kiss you first, as a sign and omen," said Bella-Yaffa.

Then Bella-Yaffa rose to her feet, drew the matches from the pocket of her dress and lit the candle, and strode toward the road.

Soon she saw them, and this time she realized that they would indeed let her be one of them, because this time they did not stand upright as a still pack, but they were gathering and coming from the corners of the field, each and every one holding a light in his hand, and they were walking straight toward her. This meant that this time they not only noticed her, but also explicitly wanted her. Here they hastened their pace. Here some of them drew near and came, all of them resembling each other in stature and dress, as befits members of one family, hewn from an ancient quarry, a family which she had known and recognized in days gone by.

They were all men, resembling in their height and in the expression of their faces that same man who had kissed the back of her hand. Bella-Yaffa's eyes were seeking Na'aman, and because it was dark around her she stretched out her hand and groped at the face of each one of those approaching her, until she would recognize the face of Na'aman.

The people treated her as she had been told, softly and gently. Two of them supported her elbows and led her across the field.

"You're coming back home," one of them said.

"I know," said Bella-Yaffa. "Would you allow me to kiss you, my brother?"

And whilst she strode among them, she leaned over right and left, touched the man's cheeks with her lips and her tears moistened her cheeks and his cheek.

"You will soon be home," the man said again. "You will have a rest and you will forget everything."

"I don't want to forget," said Bella-Yaffa. "From now on I want to be with you. You won't leave me any more, will you?"

"Oh, no," the man hastened to answer, "we shall not leave you."

When the policemen entered the yard of the summer-house and handed Bella-Yaffa over to Uri, she said to her brother, "So you are here too, my dear, and Grandfather Ephraim will come immediately, riding on his horse, and all of these people, all of us will now be together from now on, as things have been eternally, and we will not part again forever more."

From his window on the upper floor Herzl Abramson observed and saw what was happening. Then he dragged his feet and returned to the bed and drew the blanket over his head and turned his face to the wall.

The raving Bieberkraut, who insisted adamantly that his papers be returned to him, was driven away from there in the police car and then Bella-Yaffa was laid in her bed and an injection was given to her and she sank into a long sleep, a sleep with no dreams.